Poundbury and the little people.

Peter Tate

ISBN: 9798377018810

Copyright © 2023 Peter Tate

Independently published.

TO GRANDCHILDREN
EVERYWHERE

There are 37 chapters.

Prologue

A difficulty with stories is where to begin. We could start with the traditional 'Once upon a time', or 'Then the clock struck 13', or perhaps 'Modern children do not believe in Fairies'.

In Great Britain and particularly in England there are just too many people for fairies, who rumor has it, don't really like humans anyway. There are some who still think they are around. It is fair to say that this small group of believers are usually thought of as harmless loonies by the vast majority. No real scientifically minded sane person believes in fairies in 2023. More fool them is what I say.

My name is Max, there was a time that I was known as Sir Maxmillian de La Pole, heir to the throne of England, last of the Yorkists. So cruelly erased from history by that fat pox ridden, wife abusing Tudor, Henry, of whom there were seven before but none since. Praise the lord!

My story is strange enough for even the most skeptical amongst you to consider that believing in fairies is quite rational. For I was 500 years a Ghost, trapped in a limbo like existence in a strange old house. Housed in an even stranger village, dominated by that ghastly old, ruined castle, only a few miles the Chanel Coast of England. Corfe

Castle is its name. I shudder at the memory of its oubliette and mine own funeral pyre. But that, as is so often said, is another story related in the tale of 'The Curatage Ghost'.

I am no longer a ghost, I am remade in flesh and blood and educated in the current English and only lapse occasionally into my real born and bred Tudor tongue.

But I do know things you don't.... often these 'things' are hard to record in just words.... being swirling visions of ideas, of happenings, of times past, and even times still to come. This is a vague knowing of what to you is essentially unknowable.

But I confuse you! I will, over the telling of this tale, probably confuse you more but will try to make the unexplainable seem true, as it undoubtedly was, and help the children, to whom these events occurred, understand what happened to them.

The Characters.

The Children:

Amelie and her Sister Esme, early teens. From Perth Australia.

Luka and Yaya a year or so younger. From Split Croatia.

Special guest appearances from Lea and Anna who are a lot younger. From Taormina Sicily.

Grandparents:

Judy and Peter.

Ghosts

Max and Katherine.

Fairies: Lots, in many shapes and sizes.

Also includes Gods, mythical creatures, angels, legendary kings, a queer ice cream van, large teddy bears and several surprises.

Plus

Liplop (and his brother).

Chapter 1.

A strange man on a stranger hill.

To the children it was a terrible mistake, a catastrophic error of judgement by those they most trusted to make sensible decisions. How could they do it?

The grandparents had moved! Did they not understand how important the old house was?

No more tunnels, Castles, and Ghosts, just a boring brand new house situated where nothing interesting had ever happened and nothing exciting ever would. This was going to be the worst holiday ever!

Luka was fed up, this was quite normal for him, but he was even more fed up than usual. His only friend in England, Benji, was away this week so there was no one to lark about with. Yaya was more content, she liked art lessons with Grandma Judy and was always amused when Luka was annoyed, it sort of cheered her up. The girls, Amelie, and Esme were coming from Australia in a couple of days, and it would be great to catch up and have some new, hopefully not quite so scary, adventures.

The Grandparents were now living in Poundbury. A new estate built on a hill on the west edge of Dorchester, county town of Dorset. This is an old town, perhaps even older than Corfe Castle (where they had moved from), with a long and very English history of petty conflicts, tribal wars, civil wars, and rebellions. 'Durnovaria' as the Romans named it, had seen them all but these events had left little obvious impression. The countryside round the town sort of smoothed out the bumps and softened the memories, which was just as well really. There was quite a lot to forget.

Poundbury is not straightforward, it is unusual, unique really: a whim of a Royal Prince, and now the realised brainchild of a king. The land belongs to the Duchy of Cornwall. These lands were given to the heir to the throne in perpetuity by Edward the Third in 1337 to his son, who has gone down in history as the Black Prince. Famous for his military victories and exceedingly unpleasant treatment of the French. The current King, Charles the third, in contrast is not at all black, and values harmony, good treatment of the land and sustainable ecofriendly farming.

These finer points were of course lost on Luka who having had his Pokémon cards hidden by his sister was at a loose end. He found a football in the garage and wandered off in search of a game. There were no boys on the big field nearby and some old lady told him to try another pitch over the road, but there was no one there either. He slumped in a seat and stared at the curious flat-topped hill in front of him.

After a while, having nothing better to do he began to walk to it, through a glade of trees, past a curious hedgehog, a field full of teasels and a bridge over the bypass and there it was, huge, ridged at the sides and quite flat. There was a small car park and an odd looking ice cream van in the corner of it. He had a fresh five-pound note in his pocket given to him by Grandfather in case of emergency. This seemed like an emergency, he looked at the menu of pictures and bought a Magnum. He did not get any coins back.

'Been here before son?' asked the chubby, goatee bearded, ice cream man.

'No, I live in Croatia, just on holiday with the grandparents.'

'Croatia, blimey, you've got a good football team your lot. I went there on holiday once, lovely little islands everywhere, like big green turtles.'

'We have an apartment on Hvar island' Luka said proudly.

'Alright for some.'

'Is there anything up there?' He pointed at the hill.

'Not anymore, all gone hundreds of years ago, put wind up the Romans for a while but all gone now, all that remains is a good view, the ruins of an old temple and a few ghosts.'

'Ghosts!' Luka was not keen on meeting any more of my kind after his previous exciting but hair-raising experiences.

'Well not really, or well I've never seen any, some say they have seen Roman legionaries on the top, but I think they had had too much beer or wacky backy, some says there are fairies there too, but you are too old to believe in them…. tales for children.'

Luka nodded firmly, pleased not to classed as a fairy believing child.

'Mind you' said the ice cream man 'if you go to the Hawthorne bush on the path.'

He pointed to a small tree halfway up and halfway along the hill. 'and stand still for a while, you might hear the little people.'

Luka looked hard to see if he was joking. He couldn't tell but he must be, he told himself.

'Does this hill have a name?'

'Oh yes, Maiden Castle, but that's not its real name.

It was what they call in England a Hill Fort.'

'What was it's real name?'

Someone else approached to buy an ice cream, and Luka retreated still remembering all that social distancing.

'If the hill wants to, it will tell you.' Whispered the man in the van, almost mysteriously.

This chap was a bit curious thought Luka and he sort of shivered for no very good reason. Was there something strange here?

Don't be silly he told himself, this is a flat boring English hill with not much going for it. Without thinking he took the diagonal left-hand path and in no time at all found himself next to a Hawthorne tree.

It was just a disappointing bush, not really deserving of the title of tree, with an unimpressive crop of red berries, but there was a good view of Dorchester. Below him was a large field of glorious yellow sunflowers, all with their heads turned towards him. He smiled quite involuntarily because a field of sunflowers does that to you. Just above the shimmering field was the dramatic outline of Poundbury, glittering in the bright sunlight.

'Many towered Camelot.' said someone in Luka's

head. He looked around, saw no one, and realised it was just a snippet of one of those dreary old poems that Grandad was always spouting off, rattling around loosely in his head.

It was mid-August and warm, and though the bush was undeserving of his attention he had to admit to himself that this was a really big old fort. Its defensive ditches were seriously impressive in a massive rolling green sort of way. He finished the last of his Magnum and threw the stick away.

'Oi, you there, pick that up.' Said a posh voice out of nowhere. Luka whirled around and there next to him was a well-dressed man with a magnificent handlebar moustache. He was sure he had not been there just a second ago.

'That is litter young man, this is a historic place, and this hill has feelings you know, it needs respect.'

There was a tinge to the beautiful aristocratic English voice that made him wonder, for the second time that day, if he was being played with. Luka had made an art form of defying authority, but this strange man brooked no opposition. So, he picked up the stick and put it in his pocket.

'Excellent. Just what do you want to know about this place? I am the man who can tell you more than most, I spent my life researching here, digging,

digging, and more digging.'

Luka was not sure he wanted to know anything, after all the most he had wished for in this late summer afternoon was a kickabout with a football. This over-the-top tweedy old fossil with a far back way of speaking was not his idea of a perfect companion.

'My Granddad would like you; he likes ancient things.'

'And you do not?'

'Well may be about battles, sword fights, and Zombies, stuff like that.'

The man looked unsure.

'I can tell you about battles, but zombies I am afraid you have me there.'

'You know, the undead, if they bite you, you get infected and turn into one, and then your arm drops off and you walk funny, but not funny-funny, sort of frightening funny.'

Luka could see incomprehension written over the strange man's face. He shrugged but felt the need to be civil and not be rude.

'Well tell me about a battle near here then.'

The man brightened perceptibly, and his drooping moustache perked up no end. He pulled out a large pipe, lit it with a match from a box in his pocket. He sucked and puffed, till the air filled with scented tobacco smoke, quite unfamiliar. After this ritual he pointed up the hill with his pipe and gestured eastwards.

'Towards the far end of the fort there was a devil of a battle with the Romans, the tribe that lived here, the Durotriges, put up a good fight but the ballisters were too powerful for them, sort of big crossbows, you know, well when the legionnaires came up the hill ......'

Luka's attention wandered, he would have liked to see a real roman soldier, though he knew very well what they looked like. In Split, where he lived, was an old Roman Palace where tourists came in droves, and actors got dressed up as roman soldiers. Of course, they then charged the tourists ridiculous amounts for having their picture taken with them. These were glossy, shiny, sneaky, pretend, gold soldiers, Luka suspected the real ones would have looked tougher, dirtier, and only a tiny bit shiny. He knew Romans always wore sandals and thought that must have been pretty cold in an English winter. They must have had boots too he supposed, where did they get the leather from, was it cows? Or maybe sheep?

His mind did this, wander around in very loosely connected circles, suddenly he heard a loud BAAA, and something nudged him from behind. He whipped round to find a large black faced very wooly sheep staring up at him.

The man was still droning on '….and I believe that if you visit the Dorchester museum, they still have my specimen of a poor tribesman with a bolt through his spine. Must have suffered agonies but they put up a damn good fight…'

Luka involuntarily yelped and broke the monologue.

'Come on man, it is only a sheep, you must be a real townie. Not much good fighting romans if you are scared by a gentle Suffolk.'

That was enough, he was going home he decided, maybe someone was now available to play football with.

'Sorry sir, got to go, thank you for telling me about the battle.'

'Oh, well that is a bit abrupt, don't you think, but I expect you have things to do. Do come again and bring the girls too.'

The man gripped his pipe in his teeth, puffed some

more, and turned away.

Luka turned a ran down the hill, it wasn't till he got to the bottom that he realised how strange it was that the man had known about the girls. He looked back but there was no one there, just sheep.

He did get a game of football and arrived back at the grandparents in a much better frame of mind.

Grandad was pottering around in the garden.

'Grandad, I think I met a friend of yours today, up on that big hill... er something castle.'

'Oh, yes? Maiden Castle, who was it?'

'Dunno, he didn't say his name, but he knew about the girls coming and was a digger or something. You know looking for old bits.'

'An archeologist?'

'If you say so, he looked a bit weird, talked very posh, smoked a pipe, had a huge wide moustache and went on about battles with the romans and... oh yes... some poor chap with a spear or something in his spine which is in a museum.'

Grandad screwed his eyes up and looked puzzled. He didn't say anything for a while, then suddenly went inside and came back out with his iPad.

He showed Luka a picture of a man with a splendid moustache and a large pipe.

'Yes, that's him, funny old cove. So, he is a friend of yours?'

'Well not really, though I would have liked him to be. The first proper book I ever read was by him, all about his life excavating history, and at Maiden Castle in particular. It was called 'Still Digging.''

'Yea he talked about digging. So, did you fall out?'

Grandad sighed.

'No Luka, the truth is I never met him, and…. well…. he died nearly fifty years ago.'

They stared at each other for a while. Luka broke the silence.

'Grandad, something weird is happening again isn't it.'

'I fear so, old son.' Grandad nodded.

Chapter two.

A curious encounter.

Travelling from Australia to England has never been easy. There is no getting away from the fact that it is a very long way. Modern airplanes helped a bit, then all that Covid 19 stuff made it really hard again, now after nearly four years Amelie and Esme were going back to stay with Grandad and Judy.

The summer term had been moved a bit because of the ending of the epidemic so they would have a few weeks in the old country. They had been keeping in touch with Zoom meetings weekly, Judy did painting lessons and Grandad sort of rambled through a bit of history, literature, and a lot of poetry but it wasn't the same as being with them.

The direct flight from Perth was only 17 hours but it still seemed an awfully long time in a thin stuffy and noisy metal tube. Nearing London Heathrow, and both peering out of the window, they were impressed that it was so much greener than WA. On their final circle before landing, the magnificent Windsor Castle set in a huge parkland, with the river Thames meandering by, took their breath away. England has a feel all its own.

Grandad was there to meet them, avoided most of the motorways on the way home, and they came home with a small detour round the wonderful, mysterious, Stonehenge and then through the beautiful cathedral city of Salisbury.... Oh what a spire!

In the car they chatted about what they hoped to do. Amelie wanted to ride of course, and Esme wondered if she could hire a bike and explore a bit. They looked forward to seeing Luka and Yaya for the first time since their experiences with the Curatage Ghost and wondered if they would see Max and Katherine? The ex-ghosts now living in London. Grandad was non-committal on all plans, knowing that it was Judy who would make all the important decisions.

Everyone was talking at once when they arrived, Amelie said how much older everyone looked, intending it as a compliment, but the grandparents just looked a bit sad, and it was true...... they did look older.

'It's not my age it's the mileage' joked Grandad ruefully.

The house which had been in the middle of a building site last time they saw it, was now just part of a street that looked like it had been there forever. The garden was, not too tidily, beautiful, and the house seemed higher than ever. Luka and Yaya had bagged the bunk beds so for the moment Amelie and Esme had a room each.

'Let's go to the Hill Castle' suggested Luka in the first lull after the frenzy of arrival.

'There is a much nearer Hill fort that we can all manage, Poundbury hill fort, so let's just go there.' Said Grandad, stirring his Alice in wonderland tea pot.

So off they all went. It really wasn't very far at all, less than half a mile. Judy, Amelie, and Yaya all took sketch pads and Luka of course took a football. They walked along the top of the great field, skirting the edge of the modern cemetery, crossed the road to the village of Bradford Peverell and there they were…. at the hill fort.

Luka began kicking a football around, ran along the raised old walls and stared at the strange mound inside the top end of the earthworks.

Grandad whispered to him, 'An old tumulus or barrow, very, very old. Burial chamber inside I suspect. I am off to look at the old shooting range down the hill…. want to come?'

Luka shook his head and kicked the ball vigorously at the mound. Grandad disappeared down the hill.

The Fort has two remaining sides, the west and

south, still imposing but easily climbable enclosing fifteen or so acres of flat rough grass. Esme stared at the old earthwork and walked along the high East wall with its good view over Dorchester Town. The other girls positioned themselves at the end of the western parapet looking over the whole sweep of the Frome Valley.

There was a rickety noise below and Yaya jumped up pointing at the foot of the steep hill. For a moment there was a brief glimpse in a gap in the trees of a small blue train rushing towards Dorchester town, it seemed to disappear almost below them.

'It's a train, it's a train, and it just disappeared.'

'Must be a tunnel.' Said Amelie 'Under the hill. I don't think I have ever been in a train tunnel.'

'Don't they have a metro in Perth?' asked Judy.

'Aw yes, I forgot, but it sort of seems a different sort of tunnel.'

'Caused a lot of trouble that tunnel did you know.' Said a male voice they did not recognise.

They all turned to look and saw, well what sort of man they all disagreed upon later.

Amelie saw a tall man in old fashioned tweeds, with

a handlebar moustache, holding a large pipe, he spoke in a very cultured old-fashioned sort of way. You will by now realise that she saw the same man Luka had seen a few days before at Maiden Castle though she did not know this yet.

Yaya saw a short man, with a very tall round sort of hat, smoking a battered cigar. He looked a bit weird in funny old clothes and spoke in a way that seemed both English and foreign at the same time.

Judy saw a mid-fifties ish gaunt gypsy like character, in an old Shetland sweater with big modern boots, a flat cap and smoking a home rolled cigarette. To her his accent was deepest almost impenetrable Dorset.

'It would have been easier for the railway company just to put a cutting through the hill, but the people of Dorchester objected. They did not want the hill fort damaged, so they dug the tunnel instead.'

'When was this?' asked Amelie.

'If my memory is correct 1846. The trouble was it was not the people of Dorchester who ended up upset but the other people. They hadn't liked the fort before that, or the cemetery and now they don't like this.' He gestured to the South over the new development of Poundbury.

'Why not? And who are the other people?' asked a confused Yaya.

'Well, they were here first, and they don't like their paths blocked, or the natural rhythm of what is a very special place disturbed. Pressure points get blocked, time runs backwards and forwards. It is all this building you know. Too much too fast I suspect. And what's worse is they don't agree amongst themselves, fighting and fighting, there's a war on at present.'

'Who are fighting?' Said Judy with a tinge of frustration, wondering if this local looney was actually a threat and hoping he would go away.

'There is only one modern word for them…... Fairies.'

Yaya started laughing, Amelie smiled nervously, and Judy found herself teetering between anger and humour.

'Fairies aren't real, they are just made-up stories, I think you are making this up.' Said Yaya with feeling.

'I think you will find you are wrong Julija, but it is not something I would expect a sensible young lady to believe in immediately. I hope you soon will because I fear they may need your help.'

'How did you know my real name?'

Judy stood up and confronted the gypsy.

'Look that is enough, I would be grateful if you would leave my grandchildren alone. Enough of your stupid stories. Fairy wars indeed!'

The gypsy shrugged and turned and walked away. Grandad came puffing up from the valley below where he had been exploring.

'Who was that chap you were talking to? He looked like Sherlock Holmes.'

'What that mad old Gypsy?' said Judy.

'Didn't look like a gypsy to me, more like a man from a Victorian novel.'

Amelie looked very thoughtful, 'I think we all must have seen someone a bit different. I saw an old-fashioned man with a pipe and a big moustache, in some ways like Sherlock Holmes as Grandad said......'

Luka's yelling stopped her in her tracks.

'That was him, it was him, Grandad it was him...... Sir Mortimer Thingy, he just said hello!'

Esme followed him up the bank, but she looked much less happy than Luka, very thoughtful and very quiet.

As they walked home Amelie walked next to her sister. 'You saw someone different too didn't you.'

Esme was quiet.

'Come on who did you see?' Amelie persisted.

'Well, it was bit weird, and I don't really want to say, I think you will laugh at me.'

'Oh, go on, I am your sister after all.'

'That is what worries me.'

Esme seemed to make up her mind.

'I think I saw a Fairy.'

Chapter Three

Are there Fairy's?

The debriefing at home was a subdued affair. No one really wanted to go into too much detail, and everyone felt a bit nervous about the implications of what had happened. Esme determined to stay very quiet, praying that Amelie would not betray her secret. Luka was the noisiest, repeating again and again that it was the same chap he had met previously, 'what was his name again Grandad?'

'Sir Mortimer Wheeler, an archeologist, very famous in the 1950's and 60's, always on the telly.'

'So, he was a ghost then, wasn't he? cos he's dead.'

Grandad looked puzzled and sort of shrugged. Judy tried to help out.

'He didn't look like an archaeologist to me, more like a dodgy local who's not quite right in the head.'

'He called me by my real name, I mean how did he know that?' said Yaya.

No one had an answer and the group fell silent. Grandad suddenly perked up.

'Well tonight we have some special guests for supper, and they probably know more than we do about the sort of experience we have just had.'

There was buzz from the children as they wondered who it was, Amelie knew,

'It's Max and Katherine, isn't it?'

'Might be, you will just have to wait and see.'

Said Judy grimly, trying to keep some of the suspense and irritated that Grandad had let the cat out of the bag.

When the doorbell rang a short time later everyone was very excited and sure enough...... there stood the Curatage Ghosts. Everyone hugged and kissed. Katherine of course looked more beautiful than ever, though now a very modern woman. Her hair was very blond and long, her lipstick was the deepest of reds. She was wearing a navy jacket over a white shirt and tight-fitting leather trousers with gold sandal style stilettos. Judy spotted the shoes immediately and worried about her wood floor. Luka stared at her, jaw dropping, falling in love all over again. When she kissed him, he tingled, from top to toe.

I was pretty smart too, though I do say it myself. Short cropped slightly fuzzy dark hair with a well-trimmed close-cropped beard, a studded leather jacket over a garish (well that is what Judy said)

African patterned shirt, tight black jeans, and big brown expensive boots. We were the most unghostly pair you could imagine. That the children were pleased to see us was of course wonderful, but they could have no idea how much we loved them and how much we owed them. It isn't cool or English to be too demonstrative, at least that has not changed over the centuries.

We swapped stories for a while, caught up on where we all were in our lives and avoided any strange tales till the apple and blackberry crumble. Amelie was the most determined to force the conversation round to the strange encounters.

'You know something strange happened to us all this afternoon, we all saw someone different, but it was the same person, it was just out on the hill fort very near here. He seemed to want to give us a message about danger and someone needing help.'

Yaya chipped in.

'He said there was pressure in the hill or something, and he knew my real name, Julija, I mean how could he know that?'

Katherine who, when she wants, has a voice like melting chocolate, asked Yaya who she had seen?

Her description of a short man in a crumpled old-fashioned suit with waistcoat and a big, tall hat, smoking a battered cigar was quite vivid and well described. Light came into Grandad's eye and his iPad appeared out of nowhere.

'Did he mention the railway line?'

Yaya thought for a while.

'Yes, he did, something about tunneling through the hill and people objecting.'

'It was in 1846, I remember that.' Said Amelie.

Judy was worried that she seemed to not remember any of the conversation only the desire that the man should go away.

Grandad shouted triumphantly and brandished a picture under Yaya's nose.

'Was that him?'

There was a picture of a man just as described standing in front a pile of huge chains. Yaya peered at the image closely and slowly nodded.

'Yes, that is him, he is who I saw, no doubt......so who is he?'

'Isambard Kingdom Brunel' said Grandad with a flourish.

'Wow what a name!' exclaimed Amelie.

Grandad was in his element, mansplaining things he half knew about to people who knew less.

'The most famous engineer of Victorian times, he built bridges, tunnels, railway lines and ships. Amazing man, ahead of his time really. We should all go to Bristol to see the SS Great Britain, first proper ocean liner, launched in 1843, we could drive across the Clifton suspension bridge, because he built that too.'

Luka pointed out the obvious.

'So, he is dead too. Are these people all ghosts?'

He looked at me hoping I might have the answer.

I tried to think. Being a ghost for 500 years wasn't a great learning experience, but since my restoration to mortality I had researched folk lore and myth, all the while trying to make sense of my experiences of being trapped in a nightmarish limbo for so long.

'I don't think so, well not exactly anyway.'

'So that's clear then.'

Added Luka, a little unkindly I felt.

'So, what are these people?'

I sighed; in truth I did not know but there was a shadowy idea floating in my nearly conscious part of my brain. A word formed on my lips.

'Shapeshifter, I think he was a shapeshifter.'

Everyone seemed to wait for me to explain a bit more, the trouble was I was not at all certain I could. Katherine came to my rescue. She had always remembered more than I and was more in tune with those realms that are hard for mortal man to understand.

'Well, the only shapeshifters of legend that have come down to the present day are Fairies.'

The children gasped, Judy felt uncomfortable, and Grandad was rapt. Amelie looked hard at Esme.

'That's what you saw didn't you?'

Esme squirmed and looked very uncomfortable. Katherine soothed her.

'Come on Esme, no one will make fun of you tell us what you saw.'

There was a longish pause as Esme seemed to be struggling what to say. After a while she ventured.

'Well he, I think it was a he anyway, was sort of fuzzy at the edges. Sort of almost see through, wearing a sort of white toga like thing. You know like the Romans. He or she was very beautiful in my head, but I can't describe it, he made me feel warm towards him, sort of weird warm like ……'

'Go on Esme, I think I know what you are trying to say, you loved him on sight, did you not?'

Esme looked startled and a little ashamed. She nodded rapidly and there were tears in her eyes. Then she blurted out as if to get rid of the thought,

'He looked a bit like Legolas, you know the elf in Lord of the Rings, with a really special hairdo, but I think he was a fairy, not an elf, but I don't really know why.'

Luka snorted unhelpfully, Judy shook her head, though what she meant by that I know not, and Amelie seemed more than a little jealous that it had not been her that saw the elfin fairy.

Katherine took over.

'Well, these are momentous happenings; shapeshifting people almost never make their presence known to ordinary folk. There must be a purpose and…. a hint of danger. Have you seen anything unusual before now?'

Grandad shook his head, but Luka interrupted,

'Yes, I did, two days ago, I met Sir Morty Peeler.'

'Sir Mortimer Wheeler' interrupted Grandad, and Luka proceeded to tell the assembled company of his encounter at Maiden Castle.

'He was a boyhood hero of yours Grandad?' asked Katherine.

'Yes, he was, his was the first proper book I read when I was about Luka's age. It was called Still Digging and was mainly about his excavations at Maiden Castle, in some ways he has stayed with me and perhaps is even one reason why I wanted to move to Poundbury.'

There was a knock on the door. A loud insistent knock. Everyone looked at each other. They all rushed into the hall and Luka grabbed the door and opened it.

A tall man, with a deerstalker hat, impressive handlebar moustache and clutching a large Meerschaum pipe stood framed in the doorway. This time we all saw him.

Chapter Four

A bad tempered friend.

For a moment everyone just stood and stared. The figure helped us out.

'Well, aren't you going to invite me in?'

'Don't Grandad, don't invite him in, he might be a vampire and he can't come in unless you invite him.' Luka shouted with a surprising grasp of supernatural law, gained from many hours of watching unsuitable films when his mother wasn't looking (and his father was).

'I can assure you, young man that I am not a vampire.' And with that he stepped over the threshold.

'Though some of my best friends are.'

He added, winking at Luka.

Judy was flustered but it was her house.

'Er, well then…. you had better come into the kitchen, are you going to introduce yourself?'

'In good time Judy, and I must apologise very sincerely for this gross transgression of your hospitality but as I will make clear it is necessary. More than necessary, truly vital, for you and for me.'

He had by this stage reached Grandad's chair and sat himself in it as if to the manor born. Grandad too fascinated to be miffed, propped himself up against the kitchen island and studied him as if he was a patient sitting in his consulting room. A retired doctor he might be, but he had never retired in his head.

This figure looked real, solid, flesh and blood. He had removed his hat and was fiddling with his large ornate pipe, made of brilliant white clay fashioned in the shape of a head that looked remarkably like its owner. Big moustache, dramatic eyes, and pointy beard. He waved his pipe at Judy.

'Do you mind? Mistress of the house.'

Still flustered Judy didn't know what to say. She didn't want her house smelling of tobacco smoke, but she didn't want to upset this strange guest that she knew must be important in some way, so she sort of shrugged in an 'If you must' sort of way.

The guest was in no hurry however vital his visit was supposed to be. Taking out a tobacco pouch, loading the bowl, bringing out a large pack of matches, tapping down the leaf and with a final flourish lighting it.

Instantly the kitchen was filled with a dense aromatic mist rather than smoke, it was very soothing. The children were all sitting round him at the table gazing at him with rapt attention and waiting for the explanation, this was a real story wasn't it, and they wanted to be in it.

The smokey mist coalesced in the middle of the room into the shape of a cruise liner and then disappeared. The children spontaneously applauded. He smiled.

'You like my Gandalf impression? You ask who am I? That in truth is not as easy a question that you might imagine. Today I am Sir Mortimer Wheeler, famous archeologist who excavated across the Valley at Maiden Castle and, believe it or not, here on Poundbury hill but I confess there are elements of the fictitious but very real Sherlock Holmes and as you have witnessed, I can't resist a bit of the old wizard.'

'So, you are a ghost?' queried Amelie.

'You are used to those are you not. But no, not exactly, more an echo and a communication device. We need your help and, though you don't know it, you will need ours and for that I must have your attention…...'

'Now….' He puffed another image; this time it was the Queen Mother statue from the square in the centre of Poundbury…... they all stared… 'I think I have that.'

His voice was wonderful, masterful, cultured, and kind. It was the kindness that impressed me most. He turned to Judy.

'Let me give you my real name, Pomery Duro Durnovin, and my clan is Tuatha, in Ireland you would call me a Sidhe. In Scotland a Spriggon, and here in the South of England, I am a Fairie.'

'Katherine was right, she said you were a shapeshifter and so must be a fairy, but are you pretending to be good but really you are bad? You feel good but my mum always says that appearances can be deceptive. How do we know?' asked the ever-perceptive Esme.

'Well…. you don't…... yet. I think first I must prove to you my magical credentials and let you ask another's opinion.'

He stood up and walked past Grandad to the door into the garden. Everyone followed onto the veranda including us bringing up the rear.

'Liplop…...Liplop…… are you there? I have some friends that need to be convinced that I am who I say I am.'

We all stared expectantly into the darkness of the garden. Nothing happened for just long enough for us all to get restive and begin to wonder whether this was just a failed trick of some kind. Then there was a rustle, and a large hare wandered into the middle of the lawn. He turned and stood looking at us all in a defiant sort of way.

'This used to be my patch.'

Said the hare in a harey sort of voice.

'Blooming foreigners ruining everything for the locals, go way I say, just go away. As for you ……Pomery Pummery Poundbury you should be ashamed of yourself. You let it happen and now look at the mess we are all in. This whole hill is about to go…. pooof…. At least that will be an end to it, and to you lot……. serve you right…. it was much better before you humans came…. his lot were bad enough…. but at least they sort of fitted in…... went with the seasons and the natural rhythms of things.'

'Liplop! That is enough, I do not expect a lecture just an acknowledgement of who I am.'

'I dunno who he says he is, but he is a pain in my tail. His lot live under the hill, fine city once but the aqueduct started the rot, then that stupid tunnel and now all this.' He waved his paw in an inclusive gesture.

'Concrete everywhere…… don't you know this is a magical place? Play with magic and you get hurt…… you'll find out soon enough I'll be bound. Anyway, I am going to hop off. We still meet by the new fire station if you ever want a word, and I have a feeling you're going to need help before all this is done.'

Another rustle and he was gone. Show was over so we all shuffled inside and sat down.

'Not entirely satisfactory I grant you, but it will be the first garrulous bad-tempered talking hare you will have encountered. My people as he says live under this hill. We are what remains of the Tuatha, a once noble half of the fairy race, and very threatened. The forces that hold us together are weakened but we have chosen you to help us.'

'Why us?' asked all the children as one.

'Because you have experience, your experiences with these two'…. looking at us ex ghosts…... 'mean you have been prepared, as it where, for dealing with the unfamiliar, the strange, the frightening and the unexplainable….'

He paused….

'And well…. frankly…. because you are in the right place.'

'The right place?'

'Well yes…... this house is built on the Roman Tomb which was built on the Celtic Tomb which was built on the old King's tomb which is the only entry to the underworld left on the hill.'

Judy closed her eyes and tried to wish she was somewhere else; this was her worst nightmare coming to pass. Grandad had perked up.

'So, let me get this straight, we will have to excavate to reopen an old pathway of yours and then it will all be, ok? A sort of Fairy thoroughfare.'

The Sir Mortimer Wheeler hologram, or whatever it was, shook his head.

'Would it were that simple, I said entry…. not exit, this will be a one-way pathway. The old forces will never let us Tuatha past these consecrated tombs. No, it is a one-way ticket. You don't realise it yet but there is a war on!'

This was more up Luka's street.

'Who with? I mean who is fighting who?'

Sir Mortimer scratched his head before replying.

'Well…. It is not easy to explain,

'So why do you need the children?' asked a nervous Judy with Pied Piper like fears at the back of her mind.

'Only the girls, and only if they wish after I have explained what we must try to do.'

'Why not me?' shouted an outraged Luka.

'There will be ways you can help but no entry to the Middle Kingdom for you I am afraid.'

Irritated and scorned he stormed off, protesting bitterly, slamming the door for emphasis.

'Katherine you could help perhaps a little, but not the men or you Judy I am afraid.'

'Nobody loves a fairy when she's forty.'

Retorted Judy feeling scorned too, echoing the old music hall song.

'But I am surprised you don't want Grandad...... he has been away with the fairies for years!'

Chapter Five

A strange but beautiful recital.

Only Amelie, Esme, Yaya, and Katherine remained
with Sir Mortimer round the kitchen table. There was
an expectant hush as he scanned the girls in turn
and each felt a connection, but there was a sadness
there.

Esme suddenly started reciting:

'It was many and many a year ago,

In a kingdom by the sea,

That a maiden there lived whom you may know

By the name of Annabel Lee.

And this maiden she lived with no other thought

Than to love and be loved by me.

I was a child and she was a child,

In this kingdom by the sea,

But we loved with a love that was more than love—

I and my Annabel Lee—

With a love that the wingèd seraphs of Heaven

Coveted her and me.

Sir Mortimer was crying, genuine tears rolling down his wrinkled face. Shaking his head, trying to get a grip, he stared at Esme. In at that moment he was real….so real.

'Why, why did you recite that poem?'

Esme was uncomfortable. She did not know why…... it had just come to her as an impulse not to be resisted, but she was frightened by the reaction it had produced. She shrugged, trying to explain the unexplainable.

'I suppose it was your talk of tombs, and it is a sort of sad fairy tale and well it just seemed to fit in some sort of way I can't explain…...I am sorry…...'

'Don't be sorry Esme, you have a connection…...' stammered a no longer self-possessed Fairie messenger.

Amelie, confused by her sister's recital but not wishing to be left out explained.

'That was by Edgar Allan Poe, it was one of the poems Grandad got us to learn. He was American.'

'Maybe he was, maybe he was…...but he went to school in London and stayed here at the farmhouse in Pummery out of term time…I knew him…...a kindred spirit, before that tunnel but even then, we were starting to fade…...he used to visit the Hill... my young sister took to him…showed herself to him …. they loved each other…they played... they laughed…. She showed him some mysteries of the Middle kingdom…. and then ….and then…….'

He stopped, unable to continue. After a while Yaya asked what everyone was thinking.

'What was your sister's name?'

He was more in control now, smiled a sad understanding smile and said softly,

'In your tongue…. Annebeline.'

'She died, didn't she? But I thought fairies were sort of immortal, well especially young ones, so what happened to her?' said Esme.

'You are wrong… she rebelled and is gone…...' he fell into silence, everyone waited and then he continued.

'But perhaps now is not the time for the full story though I promise to tell it, suffice that you know we have enemies, very old enemies and that is more reason for haste now. Tomorrow in the full light of day I will return in different form and show you things you need to know before you can decide if you wish to help us.'

Katherine, who had sat quietly till this point, looked troubled.

'You are a Fairie, of a race renowned as tricksters, shape shifters, baby changers…. fickle and dangerous…... there can be no trusting you with the lives of these innocent children. This is an evil spell you are weaving, and we should have naught to do with it.'

He turned to her quickly, a flash of anger in his eyes.

'Tudor woman… out of time…. your superstitions are based in ignorance, inculcation, and superstition….'

He softened…

'Yet tis fair to say our reputation is no unblemished one. I would plead ti's our enemies that garnered such a reputation, not we…. the Tuatha de Danan…... children of God, keepers of the holy secrets and half as old as time.'

Katherine, whose formative years were 500 years ago, was very uncomfortable, and slipped back into an earlier way of speaking.

'That's as maybe you baffling loon. I don't know,

who are these wicked enemies? We needs much more trust in thee, strange phantom, than you have earned to date. I say…. Begone! Leave us now and return only with our say so.'

The Sir Mortimer phantom did look a little uncomfortable. Yaya seemed puzzled, which was quite understandable, as it was puzzling.

'So let me get this straight. Esme's Annebeline poem about your sister makes you sad, not because she is dead but because she left you? So, did she join these enemies you are talking about? And if she did and your tribe, the Toothy Dans or whatever, are so good, then why?'

The children all looked at him waiting for the reply, but there was none…. he was gone!

Esme was very quiet, the atmosphere was uncomfortable, this was not the fun carefree time they had all been hoping for. She opened the door to the garden and began mooching around…… the poem irritatingly still bouncing round her head. A high pitched little scream shook her out of her reverie. Looking around she could see nothing obvious, then it came again. Some animal was obviously in distress, but where and what was it?

She moved closer to grandad's shed, there it was again, definitely closer this time……and then she saw it……a little baby hedgehog…...wide eyed and staring at her…. She went to grab it, causing another squeak-scream.

Looking around for the nest, and after a while spotting an open bag of compost with obvious signs of inhabitation. Realizing the little hoglet had fallen out, she picked him up and popped him back where he belonged and was just standing up when a clear, small, female voice said, 'Thank you.'

Looking around there was no one.

'Mrs Tiggywinkle, is that you?'

 She knew this was foolish, but it was one of those days. There was no reply but as she turned to go, she was sure she saw a small silvery flying…...something…...just on the edge of her field of vision. She smiled to herself…she knew who that was ……Annebeline!

Footnote: The full poem is below.

It was many and many a year ago,

   In a kingdom by the sea,

That a maiden there lived whom you may know

   By the name of Annabel Lee.

And this maiden she lived with no other thought

   Than to love and be loved by me.

I was a child and she was a child,

   In this kingdom by the sea,

But we loved with a love that was more than love—

   I and my Annabel Lee—

With a love that the wingèd seraphs of Heaven

   Coveted her and me.

And this was the reason that, long ago,

   In this kingdom by the sea,

A wind blew out of a cloud, chilling

   My beautiful Annabel Lee.

So that her highborn kinsmen came

   And bore her away from me,

To shut her up in a sepulchre

   In this kingdom by the sea.

The angels, not half so happy in Heaven,

   Went envying her and me—

Yes! —that was the reason (as all men know,

   In this kingdom by the sea)

That the wind came out of the cloud by night,

   Chilling and killing my Annabel Lee.

But our love it was stronger by far than the love

   Of those who were older than we—

   Of many far wiser than we—

And neither the angels in Heaven above

   Nor the demons down under the sea

Can ever dissever my soul from the soul

   Of the beautiful Annabel Lee.

For the moon never beams, without bringing me dreams

   Of the beautiful Annabel Lee.

And the stars never rise, but I feel the bright eyes

   Of the beautiful Annabel Lee.

And so, all the night-tide, I lie down by the side

   Of my darling—my darling—my life and my bride,

   In her sepulchre there by the sea—

   In her tomb by the sounding sea.'

Chapter Six

Weird happenings in the garden.

Those who were not already awake were awoken by Judy's piercing scream.

'My garden……my garden…' and again…... 'my garden…….'

Luka was already prowling around upstairs and came rushing down. He found Judy staring out of the French windows in the garden room. The site in front of them truly was amazing.

Just outside the window below the veranda was a large stone tomb, of the dramatic type usually called a sarcophagus. A little deeper was an even bigger stone construction, made up of several very heavy stone slabs. It had a large single stone roof. But what a roof! It was totally covered in swirling intricate carvings. Whorls, sort of squirley circles, hundreds of them, and there was something underneath too. Though it was hard to see from where they both stood.

There were rough steps going down. Luka turned saying he was going upstairs to get a better look, and Judy slumped into the sofa feeling distressed and unwell.

All the children began arriving and peering out of

the window, there was much chattering and trying to get a better view. Amelie tried to open the door but found it locked, she looked round for the key but saw a tearful Judy shaking her head at her and realised that Judy had it. Luka came back looking puzzled.

'Upstairs the garden looks normal, it is just from here that we are seeing these strange things, weird isn't it.'

Grandad arrived with uncombed hair and looking very like a mad professor. He too had looked out of the upstairs window and seen nothing remarkable, yet this very strange vision was undeniable. His first instinct was to explore but Judy was having none of it.

'No one is going out there, is that understood, no one…. This is magic, witchcraft or something and the children are in danger, this stranger wants to drag us into something we don't understand and is undoubtedly dangerous in ways we can't even comprehend, we must stay out of it.'

Grandad sort of nodded in an unconvincing sort of way, inside he had always been a frustrated explorer of sorts and really did want to find out more about the Fairie Kingdom. Luka was not quite as enthusiastic as once he was.

His traumatic experiences in the Corfe Castle tunnels and experience of falling through time into a very unfriendly Tudor England had sobered him considerably. He was still very curious but much more cautious than previously.

For the girls it was almost the opposite, they all felt they had sort of missed out on the best bits of the previous adventure and well girls and fairies are much the same as girls and horses.... they go together.

Yaya was the most cautious.... but.... if she could just get her courage up.... was very keen to see Fairyland.

Amelie felt that everyone seemed to have sort of forgotten that there was a real threat to everyone here.... if what the stranger had said was true. Which she knew was a big if...... but she was inclined to believe there was some truth in the warning.

Esme was certain that there was a real adventure to be had and she just wanted to be part of it.

Grandad was mumbling something about crossing dimensions, as he tried to explain to himself the phenomena he was witnessing, but of course he couldn't really. The doorbell rang and gave them all a start.

'That will be the fairy.' said Esme.

This time she was wrong, it was me and Katherine. We were staying at the Duchess of Cornwall Inn and had just walked over to join the family. We had been hoping to return to London that afternoon but with this curious supernatural encounter had decided to stay a few more days, till whatever could be settled was settled. Naturally we were uncomfortable. In many ways our experiences had attuned us to the inexplicable and strange. Coming as we did from a culture and time where such things were much more readily embraced, even accepted as almost normal. But experts we were not and knew no more than the children really.

The sight of the garden tombs, so neatly excavated, shocked, and frightened us both. None of us quite knew what to do or even say. Staring out of the window a nervous awed silence fell over us all. It was events that dictated what happened next.

Suddenly, a sound like a vicious wind filled the room. All seemed still for a moment, and then the French windows burst open. An overpowering smell of damp earth…. of decay… and a feeling of glories lost…. filled the room. A sudden deep sadness entered us all…. can sadness be a smell? This is one time I think it was. Stillness was everywhere.

The light was not quite normal, a glow without sun, unfocussed, everything just slightly blurred and soft at the edges.

Esme was out of the door like a jackrabbit, unchecked by Judy's shouted restraint, and was climbing down an impressive set of stairs, disappearing like Alice down the rabbit hole. Amelie, half hesitated, then ran after her sister. Yaya made to go but Luka grabbed her hand to stop her. She looked hard at him, seemed to agree and he let go of her. In a second, she was gone too, following the other girls.

Judy rose to run after them, but the doors slammed in her face. As we looked through the window the garden reappeared, unchanged, and the sun came out but of the girls there was no trace.

'Do something, you've got to do something.'

Judy half sobbed. Grandad stood frozen and bowed, overcome by the enormity of what had just happened. Luka was banging on the doors and we, well we just stood there impotent and useless. At last Granddad spoke.

'Well, the last time something like this happened it all came out all right in the end didn't it.'

He said looking at us.

'That was last time you old fool, this is now…. we have to do something…. I mean shall we call the police?'

She knew as she said it that it would just cause more trouble than it was worth. What if anything could be done for the girls would not involve the police.

'They will be OK; I just know it.'

Said Grandfather with a conviction he did not feel.

Katherine took my hand and we walked to approximately where the steps had seemed to be. She stared at the lawn.

'Come on Max, look, let us use our old sight, look hard.'

So, we stared at the solid earth and very gradually we began to see.

When I was a ghost solid objects were often not an obstruction, and I could see things through walls and floors.

After a while I realised that it was objects in the same time dimension I was seeing. I know this is confusing but as a ghost I could not see through, or move through, walls of my own time, but I could see through walls built after my time.

Over the long years I learned how gaze through objects that were before my time. Often these images were fearful and even as a spirit I avoided such encounters. As I can attest...... ghosts can be afraid. But I had glimpsed other realms, now could we use that sight to rescue the girls?

After a few minutes of staring at the ground it sort of, to use a modern example, de pixilated for me. The outlines of steps formed, soon I could make out the sarcophagus and the tomb with the scrolls on the roof. We both began to see a deeper ornate white marble sepulchre of sublime craftsmanship and beauty, the steps disappeared round a corner out of our sight. Grandad was standing next to us.

'Can you see anything?'

We nodded.

'We can see the steps and the three tombs the

Fairie told us of. His story was true, but of the girls no sign.'

'Can you follow them?'

Katherine and I looked at each other, we did not know. I tried to think myself back into spirit mode, but the ground was still very solid. Katherine tried too; she was more successful.

As Luka, Judy and Grandad watched she started to descend, and her legs and waist disappeared. She stopped with only her top half remaining above the lawn. Luka clapped in delight, but that was as far as she got.

'Max, help me, I am in trouble, I can't go any further, there is a sort of barrier, pull me out, please…quickly….'

Grandad spotted the distress, and we rushed take an arm each and pulled. It was as if she was stuck in quicksand. For a moment I feared Katherine was magically held fast, but gradually inch by inch we managed to pull her upwards till at the last she came free in a rush, and we all fell over backwards in a jumble of legs and groans.

Our joy was short lived as we all realised that any hope of rescuing the girls was now gone. They were trapped in Fairyland with only their own wits and the kindness of the inhabitants to keep them safe. Judy and Luka both burst into tears.

Chapter Seven

Hell's Lane

We didn't know what to do.

The girls were gone, all we could do was to wait and hope they came back soon. Luka took it badly and was pacing around like a caged lion. Judy whispered something to Grandad and then he suggested going for a walk in the sunken lanes. They had done this before and enjoyed the weirdness of these famous leftovers from an almost forgotten past. Grandad took the shrug as agreement; said he had his phone and would be back after lunch.

Katherine and I agreed to stay with Judy to wait for the girls and they, the old boy and the young boy, left us.

To help you make sense of this story what follows is a mish mash of the stories they both told on their return. For they did return though not unscathed.

For the present, the girl's adventures will have to wait.

In 25 minutes, Grandad arrived at the pretty little village of Symondsbury just to the west of Bridport. It is overlooked by a famous Southwest landmark. Colmer's Hill, a strange conical man made looking mound that dominates the surrounding valley.

In the car park there was an Ice Cream Van. It seemed the time for a catch up on a missed breakfast to Grandad and they both walked over, looking for a treat before they set off. With a purposeful stride he was at the counter in no time and turned to ask Luka what he wanted. He was standing shiftily by the car.

'Come on Luka come and tell me what you want.'

But stubbornly he stayed where he was.

'He will have a Magnum.'

Said the Ice Cream man helpfully.

'Yes, you are probably right, I'll take two, two bottles of water and two packets of crisps.'

That seemed adequate provisions. Grandad returned to the car with the goodies and found a very sullen young boy. He made the wrong diagnosis.

'Yaya will be fine, I just know it, those girls will have some wonderful adventures, but I am sure they will all be alright.'

All said with a bouncy optimism that was half wishful thinking and half hiding the fearful uncertainty from himself. After some persuasion Luka accepted the

Magnum and stared at the van.

'Grandad.' He said quietly. 'I don't like this place.'

'Oh, come on old son, we need a good walk to take our mind off things, you liked it last time we came.'

'Yes, but that Ice Cream Man wasn't there then.'

'Ice Cream Man?'

Grandad was confused. Seemed a perfectly harmless trader plying his wares.

'Yes him!'

Luka almost shouted but with definite emphasis.

'He was at that hill fort the day I first met Sir Mortimer; he is spooky…… he is you know.'

Grandad turned to look at the van with fresh eyes. Mundi's Ices was emblazoned in large dramatic red letters on the side surrounded a mass of snake like circles. He frowned and wandered slowly back to the counter.

'Your name Rex by any chance?'

'Smart old geezer you are, but that youngster is sharper than a wagon load of monkeys. You better take care here old fella. Hell's lane and Sigismund's Berg are dangerous places at the best of times, and these are not the best of times….'

He slipped into the driving seat, started the engine, and turned to say,

'Mind how you go, won't you' …...followed by a chillingly wicked cackle…… and then he drove off.

Grandad was shaken, all the contrived optimism drained away as he wrestled with what was happening and what it might mean.

'I was right wasn't I…. he is weird that chap. He is something to do with the Fairies, but I don't think in a good way.'

Grandad was silent, his thoughts racing, fear growing, heart irregular, and he suddenly felt very old. After a long pause he said,

'Perhaps we should just go home.'

Luka agreed but the car did not…... it refused to

start. Grandad closed his eyes slumped over the steering wheel, tried twice more, and fell backwards into his seat.

'Being trapped in a magic story is no fun is it Grandad? It might be fun after, and the idea of it might be fun beforehand, but being in it is not good.'

Grandad could only nod, and then sigh. He opened the door.

'Come on, whatever is going to happen will happen and I fear we are meant to go on this walk so we might as well do it.'

They both got out and headed up the gentle slope along the path through a couple of fields full of sheep. Luka grimaced, he didn't mind the sheep but hated walking through the sheep poo, Grandad usually pulled his leg about this but today was not the day.

They reached the sunken lane, or holloway as they are called in Dorset. The path was in a sort of gorge twenty feet deep with trees roots curling down and round the sides and their branches over the top. Although it was a sunny day it was dim, mysterious, and very quiet……. spookily so.

The sides were of sort of light yellowy red sandstone and carved with lots of graffiti mostly of a magical and strange nature. Over the years Grandad had taken many pictures of these lanes and remained fascinated by their dramatic weirdness.

There was a ray of sunlight that burst through like a laser pointer, and something glinted between two stones at the side of the path. Luka was on it in a second, scrabbling and pulling at the stones. He managed to free the object and brought it up to study. Grandad was curious too.

'Look it's a knife Grandad, a little knife, it's carved and that. I think it is a fairy knife, look…look at it.'

He did…... it was an exquisite piece of craftmanship, about five inches long. The blade was shiny, not rusted and covered in patterned swirling etching. It was sharp as a razor; he knew this because his finger was now bleeding where he had touched the edge. He sucked his finger to staunch the flow.

'Wow that is sharp! It is such an amazing object, it is old yet new, meteoric iron I suspect…. And look….,'

It folded into itself like the finest penknife ever made.

'It's like a Fairie Swiss army knife…...just magnificent….it is so sharp though, got to be very careful with it. Keep it in your pocket Luka, I have a feeling you might need it before this adventure is over. It is obviously meant for you.'

Directly above where they had found the knife was a particularly odd carving of a man on a…. well sort of broomstick…. looking back at them and smiling in a discomforting sort of way. Grandad shivered involuntarily.

'That's him, it is you know, it is the Ice Cream Man.' Luka exclaimed.

Grandad stared hard; it was, he had to admit it very like him. This goatee bearded little man did look astonishingly similar.

'Some words carved below him.'

Luka carried on but struggled to read the script.

'Rex Mundi, King of the World.'

'That is what the Latin Rex Mundi means' said Grandad 'King of the world'.

'Is he bad?'

'I don't really know Luka; I do know that very religious people from long ago called Cathars thought him a bit like the devil.

They thought this world was a sort of hell and that

he was sort of the chief…. Well…. God actually. The knife may have something to do with him…... it is like we were sort of meant to find it.'

'Yerrr in dangerous waters you two' said a deepest Dorset voice from behind them.

'To talk of old Rex and you both walkin' up Hell Lane, well that's either stupid, pig ignorant or just plain daft. You need to watch your steps, you do. An' that blade….'

They turned to see a sort of familiar figure, a large hare with his head cocked to one side.

'Liplop?'

'Might be…. just keepin' an eye on you two Muppets, messing where you shouldn't be a messing. A couple of right Charlies out for a simple stroll in the most magicked part of the county at a time when there is a Fairie war on.'

'A Fairie war on?' echoed Luka.

'Well, what did you think it where you daft farthing? Them Tuatha have been at loggerheads with the Formorians for eons and there is flare ups from time to time an' this is one of those times.

An' you're in the thick of it, not the middle mind you as this here is Formorian country, and let me warn you, they are no friends of yours.'

Grandad's old ears were not hearing what the hare was saying to Luka, he had not heard him last night either, too old for the magic he suspected. He waited for the conversation to finish and for Luka to relate what had been said. The hare seemed to be pointing up the side of the lane and impressing some sort of urgency on his listener. Then he finished, turned, bounded off, and disappeared in a twinkle of an eye.

'Grandad, we have got to go, now! Liplop says carrying on up the lane is too dangerous, we have to get out here, up that sort of path and up the hill with a funny name and down the other side.'

Grandad looked at the 'path' and his heart sank, it was steep, crumbly, and not easy for a seventy-six-year-old. He looked up the lane, there was a sort of mist developing at the top, not a good mist, it was thickening before his eyes, Luka saw it too.

'Come on Grandad we have got to go.'

He let the old man start up the path and then pushed him and yelled encouragements. Grandad felt some youthful adrenaline rush into his system...... he had to get out of here to save Luka...... that was what mattered. If he stumbled, his grandson would suffer, and he couldn't have that.

The result was Grandad went up the steep walled gorge like a gazelle and was soon giving Luka a helping pull to get him up the last few feet. A bit out of breath they both stared downwards into the lane, it was now full of mist and there was a chatter of voices, high pitched and grating. Then there came a sound like the buzzing of a million bees, filled with fear they both turned and ran towards the weird conical hill.

Chapter Eight

Colmer's Hill

Grandad was not used to running, and this was rough bracken covered ground. They reached the path leading up the hill and paused to look back.

He was gasping and heaving for breath. Luka was fearful that he might keel over but when they saw they were not being followed the old boy's breathing gradually quieted.

'Phew, close call, eh? What was all that buzzing?' asked Luka.

Still struggling to breath and talk at the same time Grandad tried to pull his wits together.

'Shee-gaoithe! Yes, that's it...... it is Irish Gaelic for a Fairy wind caused by a host of them. Those that have heard it describe it like thousands of bees. Well! We have heard it now and that sounds like a pretty accurate description to me.'

'And me. Do you think they will come after us Grandad?'

'Don't know, it seems to me they are unlikely to do anything to us while we are out in the open like this. Let's get up the hill and take it from there...... Slowly mind you…... I am rapidly running out of steam…... not as young as I once was you know. That bit of panic took it out of me so don't rush off.'

Luka had no intention of so doing, Grandad might be old and puffed but he was big and knew things that might be helpful.

The path up this side of the hill was almost gentle and it was not long before they reached the top. There they found several old Scotch pine trees, a picnic bench, a large concrete pyramidal plinth, and an amazing panoramic view!

Grandad sat down with a determination to recharge before getting up again. Luka was curious about the concrete pyramid. This gave Grandad a chance to do some serious explaining, which was sort of a relief to both in the circumstances.

'It's a trig point, a triangulation pillar, there used to be thousands of them, map makers came and put their measuring machines on them, er…theodolites …yes like the sextant your dad uses to take bearings. (Luka's dad is a ship's captain.) It was a Major Hotine I think who designed them…… of course they don't need them anymore…... all satellites these days……. same as your dad……. he probably doesn't use a sextant now. If we had brought our binoculars, we would probably be able to see another one to line up with.'

Luka, being a boy, climbed up and stood on top of the trig point and did a circle, when he looked where they had come from, he began getting nervous.

There were tiny little columns of mist filling the valley and some seem to be congregating towards and on the path.

'Time to go I fears young un.'

Said a familiar harey voice below him.

'I've a nursery rhyme for yer…… Jack and Jill went up the hill to fetch their pale white daughter,

Jack fell down and broke his crown and Jill came a tumblin' arter,

they both went down that steep old hill, to the sound of the daughter's larter……

Come on you'll have to go on yer bum, and I'll get the old un down'.

Grandad was standing on the side of the hill overlooking the village of Symondsbury, he could see the church, and the car park. Realising that this was to be their escape route he was horrified at the steepness of the hill leading straight down to the village.

Luka was still staring at the misty host forming, some of the columns now had a sort of glow to them, and there was a more defined leading one that was beginning to form into some sort of figure.

'Will o' the wisps…... Jack o' lanterns…... they are the Formorians! and nothing they would like better than a contrary human boy to play with their pale white daughter…...see her?......you don't want to meet her, trust me on that one!...... come on.'

But Liplop was too late.

Luka could see her now; the leading figure was a pale greenish tall woman carrying something in her hand he couldn't quite make out.

She was almost transparent and did not seem to be wearing anything, yet she seemed clothed. The host was forming behind her and becoming more defined by the second, a procession of figures of all ages, shapes, and sizes. Though still semi-transparent they looked determined on their mission and more terrifying than just frightening.

Then that buzz began again. It filled his mind…... and suddenly she was there in front of him! Touching distance…...she looked at him. He had read in books about being frozen by a stare, now, for just a millisecond, he knew what they meant……. Her eyes glowed a bright yellow and held him fast, his brain stopped, and he was now a statue, inert, and rigid.

Grandad turned to see where Luka was and saw him standing as if fixed on the pillar. There was something in the stance that worried him…… he did not look natural. Running over he was just in time to catch him as he fell, lucky to be on the right side. He was in some sort of trance…… Grandad, holding Luka in his arms, looked down the old path and saw a lot of mist forming but no actual shapes. He did however hear a faint buzzing.

The breaking of the line of sight broke the spell. Luka began to slacken, and his senses began to return.

Liplop butted Grandad, gave him quite a fright, but was successful in conveying the urgency of the situation. Then incongruously a melody, played on a flute, floated into his senses. Very like, but not the same as Greensleeves, it was beautiful, soothing, calming, …...bewitching. Liplop butted him with a greater intensity. Grandad shook himself realising that he had to move.

'Come on Luka we have to get out of here, come on wake up, wake up.'

Liplop moved next to Luka's right ear and shouted something directly into it. Luka's eyes shot open, and he was alert in a moment. The hare ran to the edge of the steep part of hill, and almost pushed Luka off. He headed downward fast in an undignified but rapid bumshuffle. The hare looked at grandad in a sad resigned sort of way and gestured him towards him.

Grandad had no idea how he was going to get down a slope that steep…… well alive anyway. Around him…… the mist was filling the whole valley…... the village had disappeared leaving only the hilltop uncovered. The flute music came again, closer this time. At least he could no longer see the bottom…… so the fall seemed shorter somehow.

Liplop was now kneeling in front of him, his normally floppy ears stood up straight, he waggled his head from side to side, at last Grandad got the idea. He grabbed both ears and with one bound Liplop headed straight down the slope.

Sledging had never really been Grandad's thing, and he positively hated roller coasters, but this was the scariest…... and the best ride he had ever had. Halfway down Grandad realised he was going to die, and this knowledge was in a curious way calming to him. There was nothing he could do about, it would be quick at the end so he might as well enjoy the ride. He even managed to look back up the hill, and with death approaching he saw her, flute in hand, both beautiful and terrible at once. She laughed, a tinkling chilling sort of laugh and he thought she waved…...

Chapter Nine

The Vicar and his wife.

Well Grandad did not die.

Liplop is a clever fellow and easily managed to execute the hard-right turn needed to avoid running straight into a large stone wall. It did take it out on his ears though…. as Grandad clung on for dear life as they say. Only his glasses did not survive the trip.

Luka arrived nearly as quickly and failed to avoid the wall, banging his head quite hard and knocking himself out cold.

Grandad was over to him in an instant, using his handkerchief to stem the bleeding from a gash on his forehead. Making sure he was in the recovery position so that he would not swallow his tongue and suffocate.

Liplop was running around exuding anxiety, causing Grandad to realise that they were not yet safe. The mist was all around, it was cold and nearly silent except for a distant hum of bees.

He tried to pick Luka up, finding him too heavy to carry any distance, fortunately he was coming round and groaning.

'My head, ooh my head.'

'Come on Luka, sorry about your head but we have got to go, we are not out of trouble, we must follow the hare, he seems to be our saviour.... come on.... let's go....'

With Grandad's help he staggered up and saw Liplop waiting for him. Seeing him on his feet, the hare turned and set off. They followed blindly through the still thickening mist. Soon there were cobbles underfoot, village houses loomed out of the gloom, and the hare led them through a small gate and between some large old Yew trees.... till they found themselves at the Church door.

'Inside quickly my duckys, the little people ain't too fond of churches.'

Then Liplop promptly disappeared into the gloom.

At least the door was unlocked. The Church was very still and very dark...... but it felt safe. Grandad, not a religious man, felt inclined to give thanks to a God he was not sure existed but at that moment was very grateful to.

Luka's head hurt, he was dizzy and his memory of recent events very hazy. He stretched out on the pew, put a prayer cushion under his head and instantly fell asleep.

Grandad checked he was ok and decided to explore just to pass the time, but he could not read the printed information having lost his glasses.

The church was in the form of a crucifix and after walking up the aisle he turned left into what is the North transept. Here he found a curious spyhole allowing him to look through directly to the altar.

There was a priest there he had not noticed before, probably because at last it was getting lighter. The Vicar, for it was he, looked up and smiled. Grandad walked back to meet him.

'You look a little shaken Sir if I may say so.' Said the vicar, 'Anything I can help with?'

Grandad did not know what to say, the story was too fantastic to be believed, even though the Vicar's own beliefs were strongly supernatural in his opinion. He decided to concentrate on the human cost of the encounter.

'Well, I am sorry to invade your sanctuary Vicar, but my Grandson banged his head rather badly coming down Colmer's Hill by the steep route. The mist was so thick that we came in here to recuperate, and I have let him fall asleep on one of your pews.'

'Oh my, we best have a look at him, my wife is the local GP so she may be able to help.'

Grandad decided to keep his own somewhat faded medical qualifications to himself. The vicar made a call and, in a few minutes, a busy matter of fact lady with short boyish black hair arrive at the church. She was equipped with a traditional Gladstone medical bag, woke up Luka without ceremony, and proceeded to inspect his head.

'Nasty gash.... Needs a few stitches I am afraid; don't worry I have got the kit and will do it now.'

And she did. Luka thought about making a fuss but just didn't have the energy. With the local anaesthetic in fact, it hurt much less than he expected. Also, she turned out to be one of those people you just did what they said. There was the faintest whiff of Mary Poppins about her.

When she had finished what Grandad could dimly see was an excellent job, she put Luka through the standard head injury tests and pronounced him probably OK. Then taking a large dressing out of her medical bag, stuck it over the eight stitches, followed by a large elastic crepe bandage, which she wound several times round his head holding it in place with a large safety pin.

'You are not called Jack by any chance; you certainly broke your crown coming down the hill.'

Liplop's poem came to his mind, Luka felt a shiver

run down his spine. The doctor, she was a real doctor, wasn't she? carried on scolding.

'Very, very, stupid way to come down, I do hope you.…...'

she said turning to Grandad,

'Are suitably ashamed of yourself putting your grandson in such danger.'

Silence was all he could muster, and he hoped Luka would keep quiet.

'Cat got both of your tongues I see. You are very lucky I was here, meant to be in Bridport doing a surgery but that fog came down so fast, a real sea fret.'

'No, it wasn't'.

said Luka, unable to help himself,

'It wasn't Grandad's fault, it was the Fairies, they chased us, that mist was caused by them.'

'A fairy fret!' Said the Vicar softly.

'Stuff and nonsense.' Said his wife. 'You have a very vivid imagination young man, maybe you are more concussed than I thought.'

'But it's true, it's true.'

Said Luka with increasing emphasis and frustration. Grandad tried to signal to Luka to shut up by shaking his head.

'Tell her about the knife.' Said Luka struggling to get it out of his pocket. 'I'll show her the knife…. then she must believe us.'

'Who is she? The cat's mother! I can't be doing with this nonsense; I am a GP not a psychiatrist. Look after that head of yours, young man, I must go and cure the sick.'

And she left before he managed to lay his hand in the right pocket.

The vicar looked nervous in a very English vicar sort of way.

'My wife is a trifle direct, but she is very kind you know…...but she is not a believer …...well in anything really…... whereas I am of a more liberal temperament …... less dogmatic I suppose… er I would love to see the knife you mentioned…. would that be possible?'

Luka pulled it out and opened it. There was a flash as the sunlight filtering through the stained-glass window caught the blade. The vicar reflexly crossed himself. He took it, somewhat gingerly, and studied the exquisite markings noting the extreme quality of the metal work. There was silence for a while. He crossed himself again, shaking his head and handed it back to Luka as if it were infected.

'Look, I really don't wish to be rude, but I think it is time for you to be on your way and the fog has cleared. I am glad to have been assistance to travellers in trouble but would urge you…. well…. to not come back…. I fear you have disturbed forces best undisturbed…. Err…. I would walk you to your car, but I am afraid I am already late for an appointment. Err…well goodbye then.'

He almost pushed them out of the church and locked the door loudly behind them.

Luka and Grandad walked the 100 yards to the car park. Grandad rummaged in his bits box and found a reasonable spare pair of glasses. It felt good to see clearly again.

'I wonder if it will start this time?'

But before he could shut the door Luka shouted and pointed. Liplop was bounding towards them and stopped expectantly outside the passenger door. Luka opened the window.

'Give me a lift? Got news of your sister and the girls. I have, take you to the great one if you gets the old boy to get a moving.'

Luka got out and opened the passenger door.

'We have got company, Liplop knows where everyone is, says we have to get a move on.'

In the scope of things, getting urgent messages from magical hares now seemed quite reasonable.

'Hop in....' said Grandad unable to resist the joke. 'Where to?'

After a muffled conversation Luka replied,

'Maiden Castle.'

This time the car started perfectly. As they were driving along the A35 Luka remarked that the Vicar had been a bit odd about the knife.... to which Grandad could only agree.... but was not really surprised.... vicars were not supposed to believe in fairies.... and he suspected that this particular one actually did!

Chapter Ten

The Temple of Danu

They were at Maiden Castle in only twenty-five minutes. By this time, it was early afternoon, and the place was strangely deserted. No parked cars and, Luka was relieved to see, no Ice Cream man.

Grandad had phoned home on the way only to find nothing had changed, no girls had reappeared. He did not mention any of the adventures they had experienced. Luka's injury, or that Liplop had said they might find the girls.... in case they didn't. He just said that he had a feeling that there might be something at Maiden Castle and that they would be home soon.... hopefully.

Liplop loped off following the left-hand diagonal path and they followed him up the hill, crossing two impossibly huge trenches. What this fort must have looked like in its heyday boggled the mind. Luka almost caught him up, Grandad puffing heavily and travelling a lot slower.

On the top of the hill all there was to see was sheep.... lots of them, but Liplop carried on left towards a square of old ruins. Luka caught him up but there were just old foundations, nothing dramatic, nothing much to see and no sign of the girls. The wind was blowing, it was deserted and very bleak.

After a while Grandad hove into view, looked around and came towards them.

'There is nothing much here is there?'

He said between hill climbing gasps for breath.

Liplop looked the old chap in the eye and gave him a very bad tempered harey sort of stare, with just the faintest shake of his head which made his ears wiggle hypnotically. Grandad persisted.

'I mean it is just the outline of an old ruin…. so why are we here?'

Then he got his answer. The wind dropped and rock began piling on rock. A pillared white construction built itself on the old outline as they watched. Like one of those computer animations but this was solid, very real, and very odd.

They were suddenly staring at a pristine Roman Temple shining in an empty field. It is quite hard for hares, even magical ones, to look smug, but this one did. Grandad felt a bit guilty.

The three of them were standing directly in front of the entrance. Now faced by four beautifully carved columns of veiled goddesses who were holding up a plain portico on their heads. The temple was marble white, capped by a shallow triangular roof.

A glow from the doorway attracted Luka to the entrance. Grandad, appreciating he had been reprimanded for scepticism, held back...... fearing he would interfere with the magic.

The inside was golden.... torches were burning in the niches in front and to each side. It was not a large temple but much bigger than it had appeared from its outline, and in the middle sat a female figure wearing a dramatic dress of golden feathers.

Behind them in a torchlit niche was a life size golden statue of a striking woman wearing clothing that left little to Luka's imagination but who appeared to be pointing a bow and arrow straight at him. Seeing this figure, he involuntarily stepped back.

'She is only a statue.... well at the moment.'

Said a reassuring quiet female voice in a language he did not know but was allowed to understand. Hers was a special sort of voice, easily the best voice he had ever heard.

He took a step or two inside. The lady stood up and his brain nearly exploded. She was just so beautiful and radiated an orange light that was almost too powerful to bear. Then she took his hand, and this was the best moment of his short life. He knew she was a goddess, but who?

'I am Danu, queen of the fairies, I know the future, the past, the sideways, the up ways and the other ways.'

She paused and squeezed his hand.

'But you are injured…... that Formorian Witch has done you harm.'

Her hand touched his wounded forehead, warmth and a sense of peace suffused through his whole body. He seemed to fall asleep and disjointed visions filled his mind.

He clearly saw Yaya talking to? …… What was that great stone thing?

He suddenly recognised it …. the Sphynx of Egypt. Then she was flying on a?....... he couldn't make it out…. but it was a big insect…. a very big insect indeed!

Now…here was a shining king…. with a huge sword….and those were…no they couldn't be…. could they?

Aaargh...! A huge teddy bear smoking a pipe. Then a strange really old house with a crack in it fell down.

He jumped again when the same frightening fairy who had so recently chased him down Colmer's Hill appeared…... but this time she had a huge army ……including giants!

The vision swirled and twisted.

Then they were all together but….no!!......they were going to be eaten by lions in a Roman Amphitheatre somewhere that he almost recognised. Now they were huddled together on a black beach, next to a huge wooden ship. Danger was all-round and they were running, running ……... they were being bombed! A huge explosion and a very dark tunnel……. silence.

He woke up, it had been a very complicated and frightening vision, but he knew the other children were all alright…. sort of…. but that the end was still very uncertain.

The goddess was stroking his head. She spoke to him without speaking.

'The fairy race is sundered in half. We, the Tuatha, they the Formorians. Led by Catherine the terrible, who you have glimpsed and survived. So, you are special. We Tuatha are fading, as are they, the old powers wane but our escape is prevented, as is theirs, we need the old tracks restored but they are lost. Humans have blocked them. They have no understanding of fairy lore and unless we can restore the path, we are doomed to destroy ourselves and I fear for you and yours as well.'

Luka asked, but without speaking, 'The Ice cream man, is he a Formorian?'

'He is not, but he is an evil man without principle. His specialities are hate, cruelty and chaos....... when what the world so desperately needs is love, kindness and harmony.'

'Is he the devil?'

He felt her almost smile and sigh.

'In your folklore I suppose he is. But he is not all powerful, just a meddlesome troublemaker, goodness will defeat him every time.

Now you must go my child, take the message that the others are safe, and we will meet again before this is done.'

Grandad had sat on a tuft of grass to the side of the Temple. The hare had disappeared, and he had dropped off for a short doze without trying. He was woken by Luka shaking him.

'Grandad wake up, wake up…...'

As Luka stared the temple seemed to deconstruct itself. A faint outline of Danu herself hovered momentarily in the air. She waved gracefully and out of the corner of his eye grandad himself…. shaking himself awake…. caught a fleeting glimpse of a wondrous beauty. He wondered if he had, at last, seen a fairy?

'Look over there, look grandad.'

Grandad strained to see what was being indicated, Luka had better eyes.

'It is the other hill fort, the hill the middle of it, look it is sort of lit up from the inside.'

Grandad squinted and yes, the round earth barrow in the middle of the fort was glowing with a faint blue light. Suddenly the light went out and Luka yelped as if stung.

'What's up? What's happening?'

Exclaimed a confused grandad gripping Luka's hand a trifle too tightly, but he didn't reply. Luka's mind was too full of images of what was to come, and if that was the future it was not a comforting one.

He freed his hand and walked slowly down the path on his own. Eventually standing by the car, expectantly and silently. They were home in less than five minutes, and he did not say a word despite Grandads questions.

Judy was not pleased by Luka's bandaged head.

'What has happened here, you are wounded.'

 She looked accusingly at Grandad who winced.

'Come here let's have a look.'

She unpinned the safety pin and unwound the bandage, peeling off a little of the dressing and peering underneath, not seeing anything she peeled off a bit more, soon it was all off. There was nothing to see. No cut, no stitches in fact no wound at all.

She was confused as was Grandad, Luka remembered that soft soothing touch in the temple and understood.

'Who was that lady in the temple?'

Asked Grandad out of Judy's hearing.

He did not reply immediately but looked to be thinking. At last, he replied.

'Well, it is not easy to tell you, she was a sort of Goddess, her name is Danu.

It is funny but when I was where I was it all made perfect sense, but now I am back home it doesn't so much.

It is like waking from a very complicated dream....,'

He turned to Judy.

'Are Yaya, Amelie and Esme back?'

She shook her head sadly.

This at least reminded Grandad and Luka that they had missed lunch and were famished. Judy, pleased to have something to do, went off to the kitchen to prepare an early supper or late lunch depending on your view as it was still only 3 o'clock.

There was an insistent knocking at the door. They all hoped it was the other girls but as Luka dragged the big door open, they were crestfallen to see it was only Sir Mortimer again. He waved his pipe around in a very agitated way.

'Help, we need your help, in fact......we need a bulldozer!'

Grandad knew this was on him, hungry or not, he followed and closed the door behind him. Judy, when she heard, screamed in sheer frustration and

Luka kept his head down.

Chapter 11

Down the staircase.

Running down the stairs Esme was in the lead, Amelie not far behind and a good way back came Yaya.

At last! This was a real adventure and Esme was determined to be in the thick of it this time.

She was now deeper than that strange ornate marble tomb and the walls were grey cold stone. The further down she went the bigger the stones seemed to get. Soon there were stones so large, smooth, and thick, four five times her height, that it seemed impossible that normal hands could have set them in place...they were so close together, and so well fitted, that the point of a pin could not have been inserted in one of the joints. But they were irregular, no stone was the same shape. (Clever clogs call these 'Cyclopean Walls', named after the Cyclops, a one eyed giant big enough to build them. The most famous ones are in Peru)

As they got deeper it should have got darker, there were no lights, but if anything, the reverse was the case.

A suffuse orange glow was everywhere but with no obvious source, and the staircase was getting weird. As the stones of the wall got larger so the steps got a little bigger until soon Esme could no longer run down them. Amelie and Yaya caught up. The space they were in felt massive. If you have ever been to Gordale Scar near Malham in Yorkshire, you would know the feeling. They looked back and up and could see no sky, only the same strange radiance they were now surrounded by.

As they peered downwards the steps kept getting bigger but there did seem to be an end...... about fifty yards further. The girls began to help each other down, by the time they got to the last step it was Amelie's full height.

Esme shook her head:

'Who built this passageway? I mean this last bit; it is only good for giants.'

That thought quieted the others, they all felt small, very small. Esme was not to be cowed:

'Fee! Fie! Foe! Fum!

I smell the blood of an Englishman.

Be he alive or be he dead,

I'll grind his bones to make my bread.'

The old nursery rhyme echoed around the walls, getting louder and louder, soon not sounding like a young girl's voice at all but increasingly getting deeper and gruffer like…well…a giant.

FEE! FIE! FO! FUM!

The girls involuntarily huddled together and were covering their ears to keep the increasingly frightening sound out of their heads. Suddenly and quite abruptly the sound stopped and there was a tinkling laughter of hundreds of little voices…… seemingly falling like a mirror shattered into a thousand pieces……followed by silence…… absolute, total, and massive silence.

It took them a while to find enough courage to unhuddle, when they did, they looked over the last step and could see nowhere to go.

Amelie, being the tallest, slipped over the side and lowered herself holding onto the ledge of the step, when she let go there was still a three-foot drop. She helped Esme down and they both helped Yaya down, they had to catch her as she was the smallest.

They all fell over in the effort of catching and Esme found herself staring at three doors. She was sure they had not been there only a minute ago. A tall door, about Amelie's height, a small door, about Yaya's height and the door right in front of her face was…. well… her door!

She gasped. There was a tiny door handle, attached to a small door only about a foot high almost. Now Esme was not one for panicking, but she could feel her heart beating very fast, and her mouth was suddenly exceedingly dry.

She knew that what she was seeing just could not be. A small door was of course very odd but that was not the reason for her panic, no…. the reason for her extreme reaction was that she recognised the door.

It was her door!

The one she had been given at the age of six as a pretend admission to the Fairy World of the Model Village in Corfe Castle. Yet here it was at the end of an impossible pathway in deepest Poundbury rather than lying forgotten with a bunch of old toys back in Perth Australia.

She had of course heard of hallucinations but till that moment had never actually had one. She went to touch the door totally expecting it to disappear. It did not, it felt solid. If the others could see it ……then it was not just her, she reasoned, clambered to her feet, and stepped back.

Amelie peered at the door Esme was pointing at and sort of squeaked in an I am very surprised sort of way. She looked harder and like Esme reached out to touch it withdrawing her hand as if it had been stung.

"It's your door, it's your door! It can't be but it is……."

She tailed off into mystified silence.

Esme knelt, letting her knees get cold on the unforgiving stone. Amelie crowded as close as she could, and Yaya looked on from behind entirely unsure what all the fuss was about.

Esme taking hold of the little handle, turned, and gently pulled. The door opened; she could see a path that led into a sort of garden. There were figures in the distance, moving about, there were tiny flowers and … she strained to see and cried out as the door slammed shut and hit her on her nose. Falling backwards holding her painful beak while Amelie fell sideways. Yaya coming to help her up while wondering what had happened.

Esme said excitedly, but sounding like she had been punched, (which in a way she had)

"The fairy door, it just thlammed shut."

Amelie took over.

'Yaya, I think you are supposed to go through that door, it is your size. I am supposed to go through this taller one and well…. Esme you are now too big for your old door, so you had better come with me.

Before we do this, we must realise we might all get split up, but we must remember we are here to help…. we don't know how yet…. but if we don't…. something very bad is going to happen. So…. let's have another group hug…take a deep breath and then … well who knows what!'

So that is what they did. Amelie and Esme held hands and went through the bigger door and at the last-minute Yaya changed her mind and followed them, instead of going through the smaller door.

Through the door it was very strange. The light was still orange but considerably brighter, and they were in a huge stone hall with no obvious windows. A squeaky cross voice echoed from nowhere the girls could immediately tell where from.

'Oh bother, bother, bother!! Now look what you have done, you have come in the wrong doors, so you are in the wrong place, well some of you anyway…'

They all looked around and could see no one.

The voice continued.

'And you have come to help us! Not much use if you can't even come through the right door…. or the left door…. or the little door…. it just needed to be the correct door. I mean it wasn't hard was it, not like maths or level 30 in Minecraft....'

Yaya nudged Esme and pointed to the floor. Esme jumped, it was a harvest mouse with big ears and an impossibly long tale. Amelie seeing it too and taking it on herself to be the spokesperson.

'Hello er....'

She realised she had no idea of the sex of the mouse and was very conscious that she did not want to upset he, she, or it by using the wrong pronoun.

'Hello esteemed mouse...'

That seemed to cover it she thought.

'I am so sorry we appear to have upset you, that, of course, was not our intention. We just wanted to sort of stick together, this is after all very strange to us... and.... well.... we were rather expecting to meet some fairies, not a mouse like yourself.'

'Poodles, fiddlesticks and bumtuations!!'

Exclaimed the mouse and ran off.

They stood for some time but no one else came. It seemed to get warmer, and the floor underneath felt softer. They sat down, then they lay down, and of course fell sound asleep.

Chapter 12

Esme meets the Fairies.

When Esme awoke, she was hot, and the other girls were gone. She found herself at the far end of this big hall and next to a thankfully normal looking door.

She was not fully with it, still a bit dreamy. Without thinking she had gradually taken off her English sweater and jacket and was just in slacks and a tee shirt, but she was still sweating.

"Bit like Perth in midsummer."

She reached for her phone, but it was dead.... unrousable......she had a small tremor of loss......and slumped.... bored...... waiting for something to happen.

She murmured to herself as her thoughts began to drift.

"Maybe fairies are Australian? I wonder what Australian fairies would talk like?"

"G'day Essers, you're a bit of a drongo, sweatier than a Banana Bender's armpit and cross as a frog in sock. Strike a light but she'll be right and don't come the raw prawn with us or we we'll be madder than a cut snake. Get yer sunnies on and the magic ute will pick yer up. Nah worries."

She giggled to herself, and it did pass the time. It may have been coincidence, but this seemed to wake things up. The door opened, and the hot air rushed outwards carrying Esme along without her consciously walking. In no time at all she found herself in a formal sort of garden, with flower beds and gravel paths, lots of roses, hollyhocks, dahlias, foxgloves, and Michaelmas daisies. Very English Esme thought… so not Australian then…. she half expected the Queen of Hearts to appear at any minute and order her head removed.

Who did appear was a willowy, tall, young blond lady, she took her hand.

"I will be your guide Esme, it is easy for humans to get it wrong, stay with me, and don't eat or drink anything however much they insist, that is so, so, important if you are to get home safely."

Esme strained to look at her companion, she was so beautiful, but not quite in focus, and she half recognised her from somewhere she could not quite recall.

'Thank you. What may I call you?'

'Anything you want.'

She said with a tinkling laugh.

'But my name is Diana.'

And then Esme knew her.

A palace was suddenly in front of them, there was no preamble of walking up to it, it was there. Distances were different here… obviously.

The entry hall was very grand, mainly red and gold with lots of statues of men in togas and girls with little flimsy drapes. There was music and chatter coming from the adjoining room, as they came closer Diana squeezed her hand.

'Remember the rules, just smile and keep walking.'

'Yes Princess.' Said Esme.

In the great Ballroom, for that is what it was, there were hundreds of people, or where they fairies? Esme was not sure. Everyone appeared elegant, young too in a difficult to age sort of way…. just a bit too perfect…. elfin was the expression that came to her mind. All were costumed in a fairy tale manner, in silks, velvets, gold braided jackets for the men and high bosomed wasp waist full length outfits for the ladies. The music and the dance seemed from long ago though exactly when in the past was not easy to say.

'It is a bit old fashioned.'

Said Esme in a stage whisper. Another of Diana's tinkling laughs.

'That's your fault silly.'

'Why?'

'This is your imagination they are in, so they will be what you expect.'

An elfin man brushed against Esme, he smiled but it was a creepy 'I know something you don't' sort of smile. He offered a gold rimmed goblet with what looked like an orange smoothie in it. Trying not to make too strong eye contact she shook her head and kept walking.

'Well done.'

 Whispered Diana.

'Be strong they are not done yet.'

A stunning Galadriel like lady glided up to them with a tray of magnificent chocolates.

'The best there is.'

She said without speaking, her voice going directly into Esme's brain, and a sweet seductive… you will do as I say…. sort of voice it was.

'You really must taste one, my favourite is the Turkish Delight, here have this one.'

She picked a choice juicy one up in elongated fine fingers covered in exquisite rings of rubies, emeralds, opals, and diamonds. The shimmering sparkle almost blinded Esme for a second and as the sweet approached her lips there was an automatic reflex just to open and swallow.

She felt a sharp push on her shoulder, fell towards the profferer and knocked the tray from her hands, scattering the chocolates far and wide. The room seemed to freeze, heads turned, eyes focused, and Esme felt a desperate urge to burst into tears.

'Keep going, no time to stop, keep going.'

Urged Diana.

The room was changing as were the people, they were getting older, not so well dressed, the room was shabbier, the music scratchier.

There was a door at the far end and then they were through it, not into a garden this time but a new country.

They were at the base of a smooth treeless hill and now it was cold. Esme immediately regretted the discarding of all her warm outdoor clothing. She looked to see if she should go back and grab something warm from the palace, but it had gone without trace and so had Diana.

She was alone, cold, and in a very windswept dramatic scene.

She saw the hill in front of her was quite steep, and there were three trees on the top. Was she supposed to go up it?

She looked around again. A figure was coming from her left.... one minute it was far away.... then here was ......a stranger wearing a hood like an old monk.... grandad in his ancient dressing gown? or even Obi-Wan Kenobi?

The hood was pulled back. She did not recognise him and yet she sort of did. He touched her hand and she felt warmth, wonder and kindness. He spoke again, without speaking, in a haunting poet's voice...... she did not understand one word but knew it was wonderful.

'It's hard to hold the hand of anyone who is reaching for the sky just to surrender,
And then sweeping up the jokers that were left behind you find he did not leave you very much, not even laughter.

Like any dealer he was watching for the card that is so high and wild he'll never need to deal another.

He was just some Joseph looking for a manger.

And then leaning on your windowsill he'll say one day you caused his will to weaken with your love and warmth and shelter.

Taking from his wallet an old schedule of trains, he'll say I told you when I came, I was a stranger.

I told you when I came, I was a stranger.'*

'I know who you are, you are Sir Mortimer, Mr Brunel, or the elf I saw…. you are, aren't you?'

He smiled a sad knowing smile.

'You could call me Gabe I suppose, but Yes, of course, I am everyman…….

We must hurry, the giants may be near, and we don't want to be caught in the open when they are about.'

Giants! Esme was curious but afraid at the same time, this was a real adventure at last.

He took her hand and led her to the top of the hill. The landscape was almost familiar but not quite.

He pointed…... in the still orangey far, far, distance was another hill rising steeply out of the flat wide plain. A slim tower like building was perched on the top of it, and there was a mist gathering in the expansive valley below.

'That is where we must go…to the Tor… but not directly and we must make haste.'

He shouted out a sort of command that Esme did

not understand. There was a loud whirring of wings and suddenly two huge compound eyes were a foot from her face. She almost fell backwards in surprise.

'Don't worry it is only Meg, and she is our transport. Can be a bit frightening I admit, and you would not wish to cross her, but she is a traveler…. a wanderer …. come on climb aboard…. we need to get out of here.'

Meg was at least fifteen-foot-long, with six stick thin shiny black legs, the rest of her was a sort of fluorescent blue colour and she had two seats one large and one small strapped round her narrow thorax. Her double row of gossamer wings were quite still …. though huge… more than twenty feet across. The stranger helped Esme into the smaller seat and then sat himself. He called something to Meg, her huge wings started beating at an impossible speed and then they were off.

'Hang on tight Esme. By Dragonfly to Avalon!'

- This is actually 'The Stranger Song' by Leonard Cohen a wonderful, sadly now dead, Canadian balladeer and poet.

Chapter 13

Old Gods

Amelie woke first and shook Yaya awake. She was about to walk over to Esme, who was lying a few yards away, to do the same when the mouse came back.

'Right the big one you come with me, oh yes and you might as well come too. Leave the dozy one sleeping.'

The girls did not move a muscle. The mouse twitched her whiskers and swished her tale to point at Amelie… there was a small flash of lightning followed by a short scream.

'Ow, that hurt.'

She said rubbing her hand.

'Well get a move on and do as you are told. Orders are to be obeyed at all times without question. That cannot be clearer.'

'This is like being in the army not Fairyland.'

Grumbled Amelie still rubbing her hand.

Yaya thought the line of least resistance was the best bet and walked quietly behind the mouse. The door opened and soon they found themselves in a shiny black chamber, the size of which was very difficult to judge. It was again well-lit with no obvious lights. A strange stone rectangular box sat in the middle. Yaya tried to hide the thought, but it did look rather like an old coffin. Amelie shuffled in behind her with her head down and feeling aggrieved.

'These are them.'

Squeaked the mouse.

'I have disciplined the big one and left her sister for the others.'

With that the mouse bowed, turned, and scurried out of the door which slid soundlessly shut, leaving no outline. There was no longer a door, both girls felt a twinge of fear.

Another loud quiet flowed over them. Neither girl felt like speaking, it was the sort of silence that did not allow conversation, as if a thick sheet had been laid over them. As each second passed a little layer of anticipation accumulated, like dust. An agitation grew inside them, the dust thickened, and the silence deepened. After an age, Amelie told me later that she imagined the dust was at least a foot thick by then, they heard a shallow breath and a faint stirring coming from whatever it was in front of them. The lights had gone out.

A figure slowly formed, standing in the box. It took quite a time to become solid flesh......it was clear it was a she.... a wondrous and iridescent electric blue. Shimmering, not quite solid, she was the most awe inspiring sight they had ever seen.

She was holding a strange object in her right hand that looked a bit like a crucifix but had an oblong handle. *

As they stared, she elongated, her body, stick thin, stretched skywards. She bent over, her torso like a bridge, and her hands were on the other side of them. She whispered to them.

'I am Nut, Goddess of the Sky.'

A bewitching voice, in an unknown language, that they understood perfectly.

Gradually they became aware that they were amongst the stars. No walls, and worryingly no floor, just stars all around, above below, and inside their heads.

Amelie remembered something from the film Alien,

'In space no one can hear you scream',

so she tried it and screamed.....there was still silence. She felt for Yaya's hand and was very relieved when she found it…. they squeezed each other.

'Well, this is nothing like the Fairyland I imagined, why would a Goddess need our help?' she thought.

Yaya squeezed her hand harder. The stars were fading, and the sun was rising. There was ground under their feet, and it was lush soft turf. Nut, the goddess, flickered and was gone. They found themselves on a small island in the middle of a shining lake looking uphill at three gleaming brilliant white pyramids and it was suddenly very hot and humid. There was no sand as you may have suspected, it was a vivid green and very lush.

'Ah, hello, how do you do?'

Said a cultured Etonian sort of voice from behind them.

'I expect my Aunt Nut dropped you off here. She is getting a bit dotty in her old age. Don't turn round too quickly girls. Better brace yourself first, not something you are used too. 'No worries though' as they say where you come from Amelie.'

The girls were still gripping each other's hands very tightly.

'Shall we turn together?'

Said a nervous Yaya.

They did and both half screamed, and half gasped. There stood a giant, but no ordinary giant. This giant was strange.... very strange indeed. Yaya reckoned he was about four metres tall, Amelie thought five. He was clothed in tight fitting silken gold shirt and .... well, a white skirt with a gold back.... his skin was red...... really red.... and he was barefoot. But I have missed out the strangest thing about him. The girls stared, mesmerized, fascinated, and horrified at the same time. His head was a bird's head, not a human head, brilliant green with a long thin curved black beak and his 'hair' was made up of shiny deep purple feathers, glistening in the Egyptian sun.

'I had better introduce myself.'

Said this creature with a plummy accent and a surprisingly soft voice for the size of him.

'I am Hermes Trismegistus, but that is a bit of a

mouthful, so you can call me Thoth'.

Amelie wrinkled her brow and struggled to remember something; it came to her.

'You are a God aren't you…you were the Egyptian god of Wisdom.'

'Well, my lady I am not so sure of your use of the past tense. I seem to be here do I not? But I am no God myself…. you could say I work for them…. do all the sums for them……. try to educate them… help them with their magic…. those sort of things.'

Yaya had remembered something to,

'My teacher said you were a scribe and a doctor, but I don't know what a scribe is.'

'Tut, tut, past tense again, we are in the here and now. A scribe is a recorder of orders, events, and anything that should be remembered. And yes…. (he was almost coy) I have a trifling knowledge of the healing arts.

We are all here for a purpose and our present purpose is to prevent a trifling imbalance in the dimensions from becoming a calamity. The beating of a fairy's wing in a chaotic system can change the world you live in, so we must realign the forces, heal the wounds, and restore the harmony, must we not?'

The girls just looked puzzled. Thoth smiled, as much as a giant Ibis can, which is not much…. and a bit weird to be honest.

'Ok, this manifestation is a bit over the top I grant you.'

And with that he shrank down to a normal looking Egyptian God like creature with a Superman complex, well at least with a human but somewhat elongated head and a twinkle in his eye.

'I always said Therianthropy was for the birds.'

Seeing the absolute incomprehension on their faces he smiled, properly this time,

'I have the ability to take on the form of an animal, particularly those I like, see….'

His head turned into that of a baboon,

'Ibis is still my favourite, much better than my vulgar cousins forever turning themselves into werewolves when the moon is full. Very uncouth is my humble opinion. Lycanthropy has gone to the dogs. Do you like my baboon?'

They nodded only because it seemed rude not to. The baboon showed his teeth in a disconcerting sort of way.

'You are a bit freaky aren't you.'

Said Yaya.

'You are like something from one of my brother's computer games.'

Thoth adopted his more normal head but seemed a bit put out not to be accorded the true respect that he really did deserve.

'Toys for children, we have more important and dangerous work to do, first you need to know what is happening......'

Well, that would be a relief they both thought.... as up to now they had not a clue!

*This was an Ankh, a religious symbol in Ancient Egypt.

Chapter 14

Riddles

Thoth led the girls under the shadow and between the front paws of the huge statue that they found themselves next to.

'This is my friend Anubis, the Jackal, now mistakenly called the Sphynx.'

He said while making an expansive gesture. His expression changed to one of almost…well sadness.

'Well, he was, till he managed to get himself petrified…. turned to stone …... later those silly Pharaohs recarved his head and the future misunderstood. As a youngster he was forever asking riddles like the real Greek Sphynx, you know the one who was bested by Oedipus...'

… the girls were blank…

'oh of course in your time they teach you nothing important.'

…his tone changed abruptly to one of levity.

'If you don't keep me, I'll break. What am I?'

The girls just stared.

'A promise, of course...'

Still, they stared.

'What two things can you never eat for breakfast?' asked an increasingly animated Thoth.

'Er hamburger' ventured Yaya.

'No, my dad would have one for breakfast.'

'It is a riddle girls, think like a riddle...'

He paused, gave them time, and then Amelie remembered the answer from a nearly forgotten riddle book.

'Lunch and dinner' and by now they were laughing together.

'If you say my name I don't exist anymore.'

Both girls puzzled, it became very quiet.

Thoth smiled and tilted his head to one side.

Yaya suddenly got it.

'Silence!'

'This is worse than Wordle', grumbled Amelie.

'Do you remember the real riddle of the Sphynx?'

They shook their heads.

'Which creature walks on four legs in the morning two legs in the afternoon and three legs in the evening?'

They were soon lost in thought on that hot afternoon on the green Giza Plateau, almost blinded by the sun but partially shaded by the colossal dog's head.

Amelie was trying to dredge up something Grandad had told her, but she failed. Yaya could not come up with the answer either, which was quite forgivable as most people in history failed to work it out.

Thoth put them out of their misery:

'Man walks on 4 legs in the morning (crawling as a baby), 2 legs in the afternoon (walking upright throughout most of life), and 3 legs in the evening (using a cane in old age) ...... there is a second riddle of the Sphinx.... There are two sisters: one gives birth to the other and she, in turn, gives birth to the first. Who are the two sisters?' ...... just a slow shaking of heads.

'The answer is "day and night"'.

Amelie's attention was drifting, Yaya was staring in awe and wonder at the gleaming white pyramids.

'A last one.... This thing all things devour: birds, beasts, trees, flowers; gnaws iron, bites steel; grinds hard stones to meal; slays kings, ruins towns; and beats high mountains down.'

Yaya answered almost dreamily and without thinking:

'Time.'

Thoth was delighted...

'Yes, yes, absolutely, time. Now what do you know about time?'

The girls both shrugged in a modern sort of way, but he would not let them get away with it. He waited for an answer, it was as well that he was a patient God like creature. At last Amelie ventured:

'Well, it only goes in one direction, time's arrow, it is like those signs you see in shops having a sale on, when it's gone, it's gone. Of course, Dr Who can go backwards and forwards in her Tardis but that is only on TV it is not for real. Er that's it really.'

Thoth sighed and shook his head.

'You humans have been going backwards for millennia, you have forgotten almost everything...... time goes in no direction...... it is.... no more no less. There is no past, no future, there is just time. It is your dimension that only moves in one direction and thus fulfils the riddle. In this dimension there is no time, in other dimensions time appears to travel backwards. The dimensions are the key, and this is our problem.... the dimensions have become entangled…...in Poundbury…. the old people have clashed with the new people…. the dimensions have blurred, the physics has become tangled.'

'Er Mr Thoth, I am sorry, but I don't really understand…well anything…. I mean what is a dimension?'

Asked Yaya.

'Hmmm, this is not easy for small human minds…. the world as you know it has three dimensions of space—length, width, and depth—and one dimension of time. But many more dimensions exist out there. Your universe operates with 10 Dimensions, five through ten have to do with possibilities and include all possible futures and all possible pasts including realities with a totally different set of physical laws than those in your universe. Why are you humming Amelie?'

'Well because my brain hurts and it makes no sense to me, why does a trip to fairyland have to get so complicated!!?......and why do you need us? …. we are just children and don't know anything!'

Thoth raised a clean-cut eyebrow in recognition of a truth. He smiled wanly.

'Well believe it or not it is your guilelessness, your innocence and your innate goodness that allows you to cross the dimensions without too much reverberation, and we need you to cross at least two dimensions to stop the pressure building anymore.'

'I think you should just tell us what to do Mr Thoth and forget the explanations, we do want to help but all this science stuff, well I can't cope with it.'

Yaya admitted, Amelie nodded vigorously in agreement.

'Ok, have it your way, you are probably right, so…. let's us go and get the Giants.'

'The giants!!? Are they for real?'

'Of course, who do you think built the pyramids? You did not believe all that rubbish about slaves dragging rocks uphill for thirty years, did you?'

The girls thought it best to say nothing. Thoth walked them over to a huge flat temple like complex. In the middle was an uncovered shaft at least fifty metres square. There were steps disappearing into the depths, but these were not ordinary steps they were very big steps, they had seen similar not long before.

'Nephi, Enoch…. Idris…. you are needed, get up here and don't hang about.'

Thoth's words echoed into a hollow emptiness.

Amelie and Yaya peered down into the gloom.
Nothing stirred except a flock of white egrets which
flew overhead, chased by a large black Ibis who,
spotting Thoth, flew down and stood on his
shoulder.

He too peered into the shaft and uttered three
piercingly loud sharp calls. There was a shuffling
from deep down, a sort of large shuffling if you take
my meaning, and then a soft heavy tramping as of
very large people climbing very large stairs.

After what seemed an exceptionally long time a
huge head appeared followed by an even larger
body, two more giants quickly followed, and stood
obediently looking at Thoth.

The girls were trying hard not to scream. The Giants
were so big, even bigger than they had expected.
Amelie estimated they were at least three times as
tall as a three-story house, Yaya was not calculating
but just looking and thought the giants were about
the size of King Kong. They were wearing leather
like shorts and tattered one-piece T shirt like tunics,
in faded green, red, and blue, with strapped
sandals. True to the old stories they were not pretty.
Coarse featured, stubbled warty faces, enormous,
rough looking hairy hands, and legs like huge tree

trunks.

Thoth began to hum, the Ibis followed suite and struck one note and held it. The girls felt the very air vibrating, a single consistent frequency, they were suddenly filled with foreboding, something else was coming out of the shaft. They really did not want to look but couldn't stop themselves.

A huge cobra snake head appeared, then another, and another, until there were seven. A very long body followed, not shiny and scaly like most snakes rather it was feathered more like a bird. It stopped emerging when it was a little above the giants in height. How long the rest of it was they could not tell. Thoth fell to the ground and spread himself out in supplication crying out:

'Welcome Vasukak, Lord Nagaraja, Ketz-al-Ko-Aten, Plumed Serpent, Maker of Giants, Pyramid builder, master of the World, I am your servant oh mighty one.'

The snake god had 14 huge orange eyes and turned them on the girls, they froze, almost literally and waited to be no more.

In Amelie's head, to stop herself going mad, she recited the old nonsense poem.

Beware the Jabberwock, my son!

The jaws that bite, the claws that catch!

Beware the Jubjub bird, and shun

The frumious Bandersnatch!

Was this the Jabberwock?

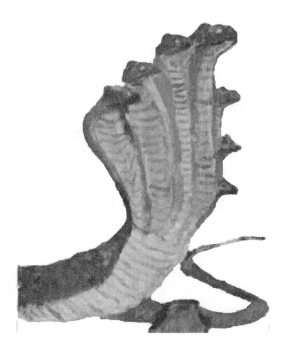

Here is the full poem.

Jabberwocky

BY LEWIS CARROLL 1871

'Twas brillig, and the slithy toves

    Did gyre and gimble in the wabe:

All mimsy were the borogoves,

    And the mome raths outgrabe.

"Beware the Jabberwock, my son!

    The jaws that bite, the claws that catch!

Beware the Jubjub bird, and shun

    The frumious Bandersnatch!"

He took his vorpal sword in hand;

    Long time the manxome foe he sought—

So rested he by the Tumtum tree

    And stood awhile in thought.

And, as in uffish thought he stood,

    The Jabberwock, with eyes of flame,

Came whiffling through the tulgey wood,

    And burbled as it came!

One, two! One, two! And through and through

    The vorpal blade went snicker-snack!

He left it dead, and with its head

    He went galumphing back.

"And hast thou slain the Jabberwock?

Come to my arms, my beamish boy!

O frabjous day! Callooh! Callay!"

He chortled in his joy.

'Twas brillig, and the slithy toves

Did gyre and gimble in the wabe:

All mimsy were the borogoves,

And the mome raths outgrabe.

Chapter 15

With the Gods to old England.

Yaya could see Amelie mumbling to herself, she squeezed her hand and caught the last line or so.

'Shun the frumious Bandersnatch.'

Was this thing in front of them a Frumious, whatever that meant, Bandersnatch? It certainly had lots of names and was pretty terrifying.

In their heads a riddle formed, they both knew it was the many headed snake god asking it. To Amelie now the Jabberwock, and to Yaya the Bandersnatch. That this was an important riddle was obvious. They both suspected there were to be no prizes for getting it wrong, just oblivion. Maybe frumious oblivion? Wondered Yaya trying to stay sane by being daft.

Amelie realised with a sudden flash of insight that Thoth had been training them for just this moment. The riddle unfurled in their minds, like an engraved tablet only they could read.

"What never rests, is never still,

yet moves soundlessly from hill to hill,

 never walks, runs or breaks into a trot

yet all is cool where it is not."

They were still standing in stifling heat of the desert and they both knew the answer, perhaps Thoth told them?

'The Sun!'

They said as one.

'Sssssssssssss!' said Vasukak, Lord of the Earth, Jabberwocky Bandersnatch, in their minds. The giants moved closer together, raised their hand above their heads and began to OM.

'OMMMMMMMMMMMMMMMMMMMMMMMMMMMM MMMMMMMMMMMM.'

The many eyes of the Nagaraja seemed to focus even more intensely. The giants repeated their OM again and again. The air vibrated to a single frequency, and reality began to fragment like a wonderful kaleidoscope. The eyes became multiple sun discs, coalescing and irresistibly merging into one. Everything was fire, cool fire, and an indivisible persistent invasive sound pulsated in their brains. Then there was a voice...... just a voice...... no form and not a spoken voice, it was almost a whisper, but it was so, so, far bigger than any voice they had ever heard:

'My rays illuminate I bend low...... near the

earth…... to watch over my creation…… I take my place in the sky for the same purpose…... I weary myself in the service of the creatures…… I shine for them all…. I give them shine and send them rain…… The unborn child and the baby chick are cared for…… I lift up the creatures for their sake…… so that they might aspire to the condition of perfection……. harmony is mine ……...it must be restored.'

Yaya wondered if she was still breathing, she felt for Amelie and was relieved when she felt her still there. The world began to reconstruct, but it was a different one. This place was very different from the Giza Plateau. A cool wind was blowing but the giants were still there about 100 metres away and Thoth was at their side. He was different too, now wearing a sort of Roman general's outfit.

After a few minutes Amelie managed to get herself together enough to talk to him, she was clutching Yaya's hand almost too tightly.

'Thoth…… was that the Sun who spoke to us?'

He smiled a kind, mysterious sort of smile. Replying still with his old Etonian vowels.

'Yes, my children that was, is and ever shall be the Sun, Aten in the heavens, may he, she be praised and worshipped……. Amun'

Amelie was deep in thought.

'So, if that was the Sun, and he or she…or it…is a God then that means the Sun we look at every day is a conscious thing, not just a ball of fiery gas, so I mean …. well, it thinks!'

'Why of course……. cogito ergo sum.'

Said Thoth in Latin but as almost no modern schools teach the old language of the romans anymore the girls of course did not understand. He elaborated.

'I think therefore I am, said your famous wise Frenchman Rene Descartes. But he would have been even wiser if he had said, I am therefore I think.'

This was all too much for Yaya, she started to whimper, and soon to sob and rapidly became convulsed by full blown weeping.

'I don't understand any of this.'

She sobbed.

'It is all mad, mad, really mad, I just want to go home, I don't like this adventure any more……I just want to go home….'

A loud angry roar stopped her in her tracks. One of the giants was pointing and yelling. They looked where he was pointing, and Yaya screamed. In the far distance they could make out three more giants, they seemed to be carrying clubs and did not look at all friendly. Even Thoth looked anxious.

'Come on girls, follow me, it is best not to be out in open during a giant fight.'

There was a long stone structure with fresh looking turf on the top about fifty yards away and they began running towards a narrow entrance. Amelie stumbled a few yards from the entrance and looked back to see the giants squaring up to each other.

She heard a strange beating of wings and then an enormous dragonfly flew over her head and swerved abruptly to avoid one of the giants waving a club in the air. 'This is a very strange place' she thought and ran to catch up with Yaya. Thoth gathered them close to him and in a loud stage whisper, said:

'It is a Long Barrow. We will be safe in there…… hurry…… no time to lose.'

Neither of the girls were at all sure what he meant by safe, from giants yes, but what sort of things lived inside Long creepy Barrows?

Inside was not as dark as they expected, the girls were panting and trying to catch their breath. The giant shouts and calls were still very loud.

'Don't worry' said Thoth, 'they make a lot of noise and do a lot of damage, but they rarely hurt each other. Big softies really but they are immensely strong if rather dim, a true triumph of genetic engineering.'

He looked around.

'Mmm, not an ordinary Barrow I suspect we have come to somewhere just a bit special.'

Yaya was almost past caring, it was all so hectic, so strange and made so little sense. Amelie was as confused as her cousin but was still just about driven by a sense of purpose. Deep down she felt all would become clear and she would be able to help to do some good for the world. The earth seemed to shake, and they realised it was a giant running above them. The girls instinctively cuddled together, and then it went quiet...... almost too quiet.

They at last began to take in their surroundings. The walls were of a gray stone and were covered in circular patterns, endless spirals carved into the rock, with the smallest circle in the middle...... surrounded by other circles.

As they looked lines seemed to move almost like

snakes, the spirals span like a spinning top and the walls seemed to come alive.

'Don't stare too hard at the patterns…… they will pull you in……. come on…… look ahead…… we will go deeper.'

Yaya seemed hypnotised, Amelie shook her, and she came awake.

'Oooh, my head is full of wiggles, what a weird wall, it is stone but alive, I do feel a bit dizzy.'

Thoth was disappearing down the long thin corridor. They hurried after him…… instead of getting darker it started getter lighter……… a strange soft white…… and there was an odour…… not an unpleasant one.

'It smells of Christmas.'

Said Yaya with her first burst of cheerfulness for some time. And it did smell of Christmas.

'It is cinnamon!' Cried Amelie

Abruptly they found themselves in a surprisingly large chamber. Thoth stopped and stared, the walls here were covered in stars made of dazzling white flashing stones.

'They must be diamonds.' Yaya gasped.

She still not able to see the full chamber as Thoth was in the way.

'Ooh we could be rich!'

Then their guide stepped aside.

In front of them, lying as if asleep, was a man, who they would have thought a giant before their recent experience.

At least ten-foot-tall, in full gleaming strange armour, clasping a huge shining sword hilt across his chest, the blade held firmly between his chain mailed boots, and it was from the blade that the light came, almost blindingly bright. What a sight! Thoth was on his knees, were those tears in his eyes? He said something so quietly, so reverentially that the girls did not hear at first but repeated a name again and again getting louder each time.

'Arthur......Arthur....... Arthur!!!'

They realised he was trying to wake him!

Chapter 16

Esme goes to Stonehenge.

The view from the dragonfly was amazing. Esme was hanging on, but the seat did sort of grip her, and she got the impression it would be hard to fall out.

To start with, the noise of the wings seemed very loud but after a very short time she stopped hearing them at all. There were two huge hill forts directly below and she recognised them as Maiden Castle and Poundbury.

The ramparts were huge. Maiden Castle was an enormous stone-built fort, and even from the distance she was she could see it was built with impossibly big and strangely interlocking stones, just like the staircase walls that they had climbed down.

It sprouted several forbidding turrets so high as to be touching the clouds. Surrounded by very deep and formidable ditches that from the sky were so serpentine as to look almost alive. It did look a horribly forbidding place.

Shuddering involuntarily, she looked towards the Poundbury Hill Fort. Much larger than she remembered. These ramparts extended round the whole hill, but instead of exuding fear and gloom seemed to fit in with their surroundings, smooth, deep, and green. Best of all in the middle was a magical city of towers, gardens, palaces, and very large imposing buildings. Esme pointed excitedly.

'That city, it is so beautiful, magical, just like in the stories, it is so perfect.'

The stranger turned and smiled.

'Cavalon, the great city, built by giants for the Tuatha.'

'Sounds like Camelot'

Said Esme, surprised to be able to talk without shouting.

'Same city, different name. Yes, you are looking at the real one, not the forgotten mishmash of myth and legend they have told you. Much older than in your stories.'

Meg swooped low and skimmed the towered rooftops. It was just so perfect, open gardens, busy squares, clean narrow alleyways, every building unique and well crafted. Some people looked up and waved. Esme waved back delighted.

'Can we land and wander round? Please …. please.'

He shook his head.

'Maybe when we come back…. if we come back…. now we most go North to Avebury. We will be flying over Stonehenge……. Exciting or what!'

 She had heard of Stonehenge…. Just…. seen pictures of a small broken circle of big rocks stacked like a Jenga game and knew they were very old…… but that was it really. She was vaguely aware that people into that sort of thing thought it very important.

Meg flew surprisingly fast. There were more trees than she expected. Most of this part of old England below was forested…… then…… suddenly the trees vanished, and they were flying over a huge flat empty plain…… just as a few trees were reappearing she could see a strongly fortified city within another colossal hill fort.

'Old Sauron or more commonly in your time…… Old Sarum now Salisbury.'

Meg headed north.

Soon Esme could see the huge round complex below. Enormous circles of stone columns…… lodged within a circle of giant carved tree trunks…… within a wider circle of huge oak trees……around all of this were broad, clean, flat, roads…… radiating out from the periphery. On the fringes of this almost unbelievably complex pattern were a series of large shed like buildings.

Nearing the centre were a group of what appeared to be freshly dug circular ditches and…... in the actual centre…... was an impressive, perfect, stone circle……. hardly recognisable as the broken-down ruin she had seen pictures of.

Meg flew down and hovered over the stones.

The outer circle was unbroken, Esme counted 30 standing stones capped by 30 lintel…... inside was a circle of 30 uncapped smaller stones……. and then there were four batches of two gigantic, capped stones, (called trilithons). Dividing the inner stone were two very tall stones. Everything was sharp edged and smooth, as if carved very recently. Esme furrowed her brow.

'Mr Gabe, when are we? If you see what I mean?'

'Just Gabe…... in your time measurement about quarter of a million BC……. a time some people still call…… the first time…… Zep Tepi…… that is what the Egyptians called it.'

'Gosh that seems such a long time ago….'

'Only to you…… those rocks that form the henge…. they are only 100 million years old…... even the Earth is quite young……... only 5000 million years old…… the universe is quite old at 15 billion years.'

Esme struggled and failed to get her head round the enormous scale of time. It is something none of us can really do…... even those, like me, trapped as a spirit for 500 years.

Suddenly something gigantic and grey black flew up past them, missing them by only a few feet. Meg swerved, flew higher, but another object whizzed by. Esme looked down, huge rough looking giants were picking up the stones and throwing them….at them!

'Hold on!' cried Gabe.

And Meg went into a deep dive, another stone whistled by, even closer this time, the draught of its passing caused Meg to wobble a bit. They were near the ground now, rapidly approaching a long low grass topped construction.

Esme, just for a second, caught a glimpse of two girls. For a moment she couldn't let herself believe it, but no, as she stared it was very definitely her own sister Amelie and Yaya, running towards the entrance…. with several large giants in pursuit throwing boulders. No sooner had she glimpsed them…... they were gone. And Meg was heading north, leaving the angry giants behind.

Soon they were over another, quite unbelievably, even larger stone circle. This time with huge ditches surrounding it. The stones were irregularly shaped but very large. Seven magnificent standing obelisks stood like sentinels in the centre. Meg flew round and settled on the top of a large white chalk stepped pyramid in the middle of a deep black lake…… about a mile from the circle.

'I saw Amelie and Yaya being chased into that long building thing; will they be, ok?'

'They are fine, my brother Michael is with them.'

Esme felt relieved and knew it was true, Gabe was just that sort of person who you know tells the truth.

'What is this pointy hill we are on? It is very steep.'

'In your time they call it Silbury Hill. In the Dark Ages it was called Merlin's Mount, and now? It marks the source of the river Thames and is an energy collector. It is part of a grid that circles and recircles the Earth......can you feel it?'

She could...... a warm sort of tingling energy seemed to be running through her body......some instinct made her close her eyes and she saw stars....... not the sort when you bump your head...... real stars...... Three of them in a line and below an even brighter star!

When she opened her eyes, it was dark and there was that same vision but now in front of her in the night sky. In a frail little awed voice, she asked.

'What are those stars?'

'Orion's Belt...... pointing to Sirius...... the Dog Star...... home of Horus and I am one of his....... We are stood upon his transmitter.'

'Wasn't he a God.'

'No, my dearest Esme, it is not that he wasn't...... he is, and you would call him a God....... and I would call him...... Father. A Sirian, a star child...... leader of the Annunaki...... maker of the Nephilim and creator of humanity.'

'Gosh....'

Even as she said it, she knew it seemed, well a little inadequate. But it is not every day you get to think about the sheer enormity of the reality of Gods.

'Er, am I going to see him?'

Gabe smiled and shook his head.

'No that would be too much, even for me Horus can be overwhelming, but you are under his protection.'

'What about the giants? Are they going to come this way?'

'No, they built this pyramid hill and the Avebury complex, but they are forbidden here now. Far too destructive. Very good at digging and throwing large stones but I am afraid they are very dim and not very good at taking orders. Now...... we have come to pick up a passenger. She might be a trifle damp.'

Esme looked down at the shiny black lake and could see nothing to begin with. But as her eyes adjusted to the darkness...... she could just make out an arm...... covered in a loose white gauze...... waving....at her? Words came in her head,

'Clothed in white samite, mystic, wonderful...'

Meg nestled down, Gabe nodded, pointed to some steps and Esme climbed off. She felt pulled towards the water and headed down the steep steps to the edge.

The arm was clearer now and was waving what

seemed a small shining sword. Esme hypnotised, abandoned caution, walked straight into the water and towards the arm. She just knew that is what she was meant to do.

Not till the water was chest height could she reach the outstretched other arm, but she felt no fear. Her hand was grasped, and a pale exquisite lady appeared in front of her out of the lake.

Her hair so black that her head was almost a skull in the blackness of the water. The figure indicated that

Esme was to take the sword, and she did…… by the hilt.

It was much lighter than she had expected and gave off its own unearthly light.

'To the shore my brave little one, you have passed a test, you are courageous, and I fear you might need to be.'

She gripped her hand and led her to the shore and serenely up the pyramid stairs. Esme gripping both her hand and the sword very tightly. At the top she bowed her head towards Gabe.

'I am Morgana le Fay; Lady of the Lake, and we must go to Arthur.'

Chapter 17

Arthur looking over Avalon.

Yaya and Amelie stared at this shining figure, unsure who he was and not clear if he was dead or just sleeping in some sort of trance.

He did not look dead, though he was a bit ghostly they said later, (though probably trying not to hurt my feelings). Their companion seemed upset and amazed.

Both emotions were unexpected to the girls who had seen him as unflappable and somewhat god like. He was shaking his head.

'I thought you gone, lost…. but here I find you as if sleeping… my King, my King.'

'King Arthur?? He is a legend or something.' Said Yaya

Amelie was struggling to remember old Disney movies and bits of the story that Grandad had gone on about once.

'The Sword in the Stone!! Yes, that was it, the magic sword, Excaler something.'

'Excalibur!' Yaya completed.

She knelt at feet of the figure of the King and

touched the sword!

There was a crash of something like thunder…. the sword flashed even brighter…… they were surrounded very briefly by a swirling palette of colours……, patterns and then…… total blackness.

No one said anything for what seemed like ages. Yaya began to cry,

'I broke the spell, I am sorry, really sorry I didn't mean to do anything bad…. I'm sorry.'

After a while the silence was broken by a faint metallic rustling sort of sound……. followed by a clatter of something large falling…… then an angry oath. Suddenly there was a light…… a sort of candlelight…… but it was coming from their companion's finger!

'A magic flame!' exclaimed Yaya.

What the flame illuminated really was amazing……. The large king was bending to pick up the sword and, until the light arrived, was having difficulty finding the hilt.

He turned in apparent surprise looking in the direction of the light which partly blinded him for a moment. Peering into the gloom and unable to make out who was with him in the chamber. The girls were very nervous, their companion, unreassuringly, seemed even more nervous, standing between them...... raising his arm to give more light.

'What manner of sorcery is this? ....is that you Merlin?'

Said a deep voice in a wonderful language fully of twirly bits and images that they had never heard before but understood perfectly.

'Yes sire, tis I and two companions. One of whom broke your entrapment as only a young innocent could.'

Arthur finally grasped his sword firmly and it lit up. Amelie was reminded of Luke Skywalker's lightsaber, but it didn't make the buzzing noise. She looked up at their guide.... he had changed again.... quite obviously a wizard now with appropriate large pointed black hat ...... a huge floppy brim and of course...... clutching the obligatory gnarled tall staff...... in his unlit hand.

'Merlin?'

She thought and said aloud without thinking. Yaya echoed it.

'Merlin......you were a famous magician from old stories and cartoons.'

'I think my child you will find I still am…. I am not… is your past tense. I am here next to you…. you really must improve your grammar.'

'But you told us you were Thoth or Hermes thingummy gistus. So, who really are you?'

'Grammar again, 'so who are you really?'

Arthur was coming to his senses but confused by the trivial banter in front of him. He was an awesome sight, now stood before them at least three metres tall, in full shining armour and delicate patterned chain mail.

He had a high pointed silver helmet circled by a multi jeweled crown and with wings sprouting from each side.

Talking of wings, Amelie was unsure that she was seeing correctly, but he seemed to have almost transparent, but definitely there, real angel like wings tucked in behind him.

Handsome in a craggy Hollywood superhero sort of way, a chiseled jaw and shining green eyes completed the look. Staring at the small company he became unbalanced, then staggered, almost fell, but used his shield to steady himself.

'I am not quite rid of this damnable spell.'

He looked directly at Yaya.

'I must thank you for freeing me from Mordred's web.'

Yaya not quite knowing the correct response, was feeling a little unsure about getting credit for something she was quite unaware of doing, half curtsied and smiled a shy smile.

'Who was Mordred?' she wondered.

She didn't want to meet him that was for sure. She believed these were just thoughts in her head but Thoth…...now Merlin…… replied as if she had spoken out loud.

'King of the Formorians. Wielder of the Sword of Light and sworn enemy of my liege lord, Arthur who holds the even mightier Excalibur. Arthur is king of the Tuatha, The shining one, ruler of Camelot and guardian of the vale of Avalon.'

Something jogged in Amelie's memory.

'Avalon? Valley of apples……I remember there is a music festival there…er…Glastonbury Festival…. yes, that's it…. My mum always wanted to go but never managed it…. best bands in the world play there….'

She looked up at Arthur who had the air of someone who had gone to sleep in one place and woken up in another. It occurred to her that of all this mighty King's likely attributes playing a Fender Stratocaster in damp field to bunch of rich hippies was unlikely to be one of them.

She too half smiled at the mighty figure this time in an apologetic.

'I am sorry to be thinking silly trivial thoughts in front of such a magnificent King' sort of way.

'The Giants are loose Sire, but I have just arrived in this place myself so am not entirely sure of where we are.'

Arthur could feel a headache coming on.

'Merlin you are my guide, my physician, and my sorcerer. If you don't know then what hope have we!'

Amelie whispered to Yaya.

'Look, he has got wings, do you think he is an angel?'

Yaya thought the direct approach was the best.

'Mr King, Amelie here wonders if you are an angel because you have wings?'

Arthur appeared to have forgotten about the presence of the girls and did a double take at the question from this frail little feminine voice from the gloom. He looked to Merlin for aid.

'Arthur is one of the last of the direct descendants of the Annunaki, so yes he does have wings, but he is above the angels, they are his messengers.'

Clear as mud. The girls held each other's hand.

'So, is he a God?' whispered Yaya.

'Sort of.' Replied Merlin enigmatically.

'Well, I don't feel like a god just at this moment.' Grumbled Arthur almost to himself.

There was a strange whizzing noise like the beating of huge wings and then a light was advancing towards them up the corridor. Arthur raised his huge sword, and this lit up the advancing company.

'Esme!' cried Amelie.

And there she was!... striding purposively towards them brandishing her smaller sword over her head to light the path.

Behind her was an ethereal pale lady who seemed almost to be floating rather than walking followed by a figure who seemed a lot like Thoth or Merlin or whoever. Seeing the impressive huge, armored figure, Esme hesitated, and Morgana swept past.

'You are free!' she said.

Sweeping up to Arthur and kissing him full on the lips. He seemed almost embarrassed, and half pushed her away. She smiled kissed him again for fun and turned to look at the girls. She stared hard at them. Amelie tried to break the tension.

'Yaya accidently broke the spell and King Arthur woke up.'

Morgana ignored her and looked across at Merlin. She smiled.

'Ah you old villain, it is the Merlin disguise again, well I have got your brother here so you can't fool him.'

The two strangers looked at each other.

Merlin said,

'Hello Gabriel.'

'Hello Michael.' Said his brother.

Amelie suddenly understood.

'Oh my gosh…… YOU are the angels…… and I thought this was about fairies!'

Chapter 18.

To Glastonbury

Morgana seemed to take over, despite being in the presence of a godlike king and two archangels.

'We must fly to Glastonbury Tor, then gather our forces and prepare to repel the wicked Mordred.'

'But how will that get us back home and fix the problem? whatever the problem is.' Wondered Esme aloud.

Morgana smiled at her. A sort of eerie unnerving smile.

'Well, you children have done the hard work, waking Arthur should make it much easier to restore the balance, but we must keep the Formorians in check, so we need the magic of The Tor. Mordred is sure to know that things are stirring, he will feel it in the vibes so we must make haste. Arthur, can you fly? .... I don't think our Dragonfly will take your weight, or yours Merlin Michael ......whatever.'

They turned and hurried back down the passageway. In the open-air Meg spotted all of them including the huge King. She stirred restively her front leg pawing the ground and emitting a cross sort of buzzing sound.

'It's all right old girl, just three children and a light lady, we will travel by our own steam…… quite a sight I imagine.'

Said Gabriel calming her somewhat.

The children and Morgana climbed up on the correct number of seats that magically appeared and without ado Meg took off.

They looked down, fixed on the trio below them. Suddenly Arthur sheathed his great sword, unfolded his huge silver wings, flapped a couple of times to test them and then took off.

Gabriel and Michael suddenly looking very like real angels, unfurled their great white wings and followed him.

As they flew higher over the vast great flat plain, in the distance a hill with a very tall tower was visible. Meg was heading straight for it.

Esme, sitting at the back, was still holding her sword as, unlike Arthur, she had nowhere to put it. She pushed it down the side of the seat and tried to wedge against her leg, but it slipped down out of reach.

'Oh Bother….'. She hoped she wouldn't need it till they landed.

After only a few minutes the strange hill became clearer, it was stepped in four clear layers. Amelie though it looked like a cake with a candle on the top. For this was the famous Glastonbury Tor.

Underneath them, a mile or two from the Tor they could see several shining rectangles. After a while Yaya realized what they were.

'Look, they are soldiers…… oh my……it is an army.'

Amelie looked down too. She could see puffs of something and then something large and round whizzed past…… too close for comfort.

'Cursed Ballistae!' cried Morgana,

'Beware the threads! They will ensnare us. Esme unsheathe your sword we might need it.'

Another ballista flew nearby, this one exploded and a mass of wire like tentacles spread out rapidly. One caught on Meg's tail, and then another, she began to struggle.

Esme scrabbled to reach with her sword, and with a variety of contortions at last grasped it, but she was too far away from the ensnaring threads to cut any of them.

The dragonfly stalled and started spinning. Esme, with quite a struggle, managed to cut two of the cords and Meg steadied herself. The mass of evil tentacles fell away, but Morgana's scream jolted Esme from her triumph.

Amelie and Yaya were gone!

'Use your magic, use your magic.'

Yelled Esme is a panic.

Morgana was looking downwards but could see nothing. Another ballista whizzed by. Meg took drastic evasive action, and darted forwards as fast as she could fly. Esme stared into the blackness below and could see no sign of the girls. A terrible sadness enveloped her.

In a just a few minutes Meg had landed on the strange hill behind the shining white tower. Esme was in shock; this was supposed to be an adventure with a little bit of danger but not this!

To lose Amelie and Yaya was not what she

expected. Of course, you know that they were both ok...... but Esme did not.

She was sobbing uncontrollably when the huge shining King Arthur alighted beside her. Morgana too looked distraught. She had lost her etherealness and just looked like a very anxious woman of indeterminate age. Arthur was shaking his head.

'Where did those two go? Merlin and his brother, just disappeared when they started shooting those balls at us.'

Esme had a moment of hope...... no angels meant they were doing something...... perhaps they had caught the girls? After all they were.... well.... Angels.

She at last had hope but no certainty. Behind her several soldiers were running up the steep path, when they saw Arthur, they fell to their knees and chanted.

'Arthur.... King.... Arthur......King!'

Arthur played to the gallery, unsheathing Excalibur which gave off a brilliant light that reflected off the white tower behind him.

'I am back, your King! We will defeat Mordred and restore balance to our Earth.'

Morgana was peering down to the plain below. It was not a reassuring site. The army spread out below was vast, she guessed at least 50,000. Mostly dressed in shining black armour plate.

In the front were a collection of giants, at least 30 of them but in front of that was a little white hut like thing that Morgana was having difficulty recognising. She waved her hand and magically projected an image of this object onto the white tower.

Esme looked and recognised it at once. It was an ice cream van, one that Luka would have recognised too. On the side was Mundi's Ice Creams with the swirling flame motif as before.

'What diabolical magic is this?' shouted Arthur to no one in particular.

Morgana was frowning and took it upon herself to reply.

'It's Mundi, King Mundi, he is behind all the trouble in the world. He has allied himself with your enemy Mordred.'

Arthur was visibly annoyed,

'I know him! He is Beelzebub!'

He called out for a spear and was given a huge,

long shafted javelin by two soldiers who struggled to lift it.

Arthur grabbed it as if it were a matchstick and in one swift motion threw it with amazing speed at the van which was at least half a mile away.

The spear hit the van exactly at the U in Mundi, a door opened and a little man with a goatee beard scuttled out and shook his fist at Arthur. Then just as suddenly there was a puff of smoke and he disappeared.

The smoke spread became a dense mist and rapidly covered the army below, the giant's heads were the last to disappear. It was all very still and very eerie.

Morgana waved her hand as if casting a spell, but the valley carried on filling with mist. Then something very strange happened, as if all this was not strange enough. On the top of the mist a mirage developed, a whole city slowly formed as if in a photograph.

'Fata Morgana.' Whispered Arthur.

Esme who was still partly in shock just stared at the developing image.

There was something eerily familiar about this vision of strange architecture. Here was a large central square, full of very imposing buildings with ornate carvings and one with a high striking brightly lit tower. An illuminated statue of someone wearing a funny hat, the figure seemed to be shaking, in danger of toppling. It was all on a hill and seemed arranged as a series of weird villages coming together to make up the whole.

Of course, how could she be so dense!

It was Poundbury.

Chapter 19

Yaya meets a Goddess.

Falling off a giant dragonfly flying a mile high is not one of those pastimes to be strongly recommended.

Neither Amelie nor Yaya thought very much of the experience. It did help though to have their very own guardian angels nearby, especially below them! Though, it has to be admitted, this is not the first thought that ran through their heads. That went something like:

'Aaaaaaaargh...... I'm going to die......too young.... aaaaargh etc.'

It was Gabe that caught Amelie, rather too near the ground for peace of mind. Not before Amelie had wisely accepted her fate...... and passed out.

Yaya was both luckier and unluckier depending on how you see it.

She managed to keep screaming till Michael Merlin Thoth swooped underneath her using his huge white angel wings to catch her fall.

The angel had not in fact used his wings for simply ages so was a trifle rusty. He totally failed to calculate the appropriate closing speed sufficiently accurately ......with the result that Yaya hit her head

on his head! ……. and was knocked out cold……
before a somewhat genuinely stunned angel could
actually catch her and at last deposit her
somewhere safe.

He fell through a couple of dimensions that he had
not intended to and suddenly found himself standing
is a small clearing in a what seemed a big forest.

'Oh bother, bother, bother, this is really going to
mess things up. Now where I am I?'

It is probably time to get a little worried when even a
Supreme Archangel doesn't know where they are.

There was a very glamorous lady who did not
seemed to be wearing too much, which in normal
circumstances might have cheered him up, had she
not been pointing an arrow squarely at his chest.

He was still holding an out for the count Yaya, so
had no free arm to give a peace gesture.

'Well, that was certainly an entrance……wow that is
quite an egg you've got on your head. I suppose
you are going to tell me that the other chap looks
worse. Anyway, it looks like you got the girl.' Said
the lady.

He laid Yaya down on the soft mossy grass. Felt his
head, there certainly was a large bump on his
forehead, but Angels heal quickly and as he turned

to look at his adversary it was already gone.

Her bowstring was still pulled taught, and the arrow still pointed at him.

'Do I know you?' she asked in a manner he wished had been a trifle more gentle.

He decided to be angelic as the easiest way of defusing the tricky situation. A bright halo appeared round his head, and he adopted a beatific expression of peace and love.

'Oh, one of those….'

He was disappointed at the response.

'Well two can play at that game.'

She doubled in stature, turned golden, radiated light and she became so bright he had to cover his eyes.

'I am the Goddess Artemis, Bast and Diana, for the Greek, the Egyptian and the Roman.'

The bright light seemed to wake Yaya.

She stirred, opened her eyes, and sat up staring at this vision of terrifying womanhood in front of her.

Her head was hurting, and she rubbed it, the goddess saw this gesture, shrank back to normal size and seeing no threat put her bow down. Walking over to Yaya she touched her head, and which felt absolutely wonderful.

'So, you rescue children by banging them on the head!'

 She narrowed her eyes.

'But I do recognise you, but not as this feathered angel, your bird is the Ibis is it not? You are Thoth.'

He smiled,

'And you, not in the guise I know well.'

Bast smiled a feline smile, and her clothes became colorful and tight fitting in the Egyptian style, her face became that of a black panther, and she sprouted a long swishing black tale.

Yaya was trying to work out what was happening.

She tried to go through the last things she remembered…... the shining Arthur…… climbing on the huge dragonfly and then…. yes…. the aerobatics and then the falling…... and the screaming…. she shivered.

So, Thoth had saved her! On this realisation she stood up and hugged his leg, being the only piece of him she could reach.

'You saved me Mr Thoth, you saved me. Thank you…. thank you.'

'You always did have that effect on the ladies.'

Bast sighed.

'Now what is to be done? There is obviously some disturbance in the dimensions, and this child......'

'My name is Julija Bozic Vittorio, but everyone calls me Yaya.'

'Well, whatever...... You are out of your place and time, and I presume need restituting and this clever man here is too busy, so if you want a job doing well ask a woman, is that not true? Yaya.'

'It is true I am needed elsewhere, but all the lines are jamming together, stuck above, around and under old Camelot and this brave child is part of the attempt to restore the balance. She has been very brave for one of her kind.'

'Well off you go then on your errands, this child will be safe with me and in good time I will return her to where she should be. Just who are you supposed to be at this moment?'

'Merlin.'

'Oh, you are with Arthur are you, in his eternal battle with the Lord of Darkness, Beelzebub, your old friend Seth, in whatever disguise he takes on. Good luck there, he is a devious unpleasant character.'

The angel smiled in a 'you can say that again' sort of smile and disappeared.

'Well Yaya time for another adventure. It may not be easy, and it may be frightening, so you must be brave.'

Yaya was not sure she liked the sound of that, but it seemed peevish to be ungrateful in the circumstances. She took the hand of the cat like Goddess; it was a hand, but it felt like a smooth furry paw.

She turned her head to look up at her, and yes, she still had a black panther face. Bast looked at her and there was warmth in the green eyes, but Yaya could not read the facial expression. Do cats smile? She wondered. Perhaps only when they are about to eat you?

Yaya was trying to work out where she was. This was not easy as everything kept changing. There were no boundaries, as if everything was in soft focus, she wasn't even sure if they were moving. I think she realized for the first time what it might feel like to be a ghost.

Bast sort of purred into her head, soundlessly but anticipating her question.

'Do not worry my child we are not far away, but you are on a nameless quest are you not?'

Yaya was too confused to reply.

'I see your mind all muddled but full of kindness and hope, it is our turn to help you understand. Here is a place you know.'

And suddenly they were seated in the open air, and she recognised the snow-coloured smoking mountain now in front of her. It was Etna, and she was in the temple complex of Taormina, only this time it was not a ruin but like new, magnificent, awe inspiring and somehow comforting.

They were seated in the middle of a huge crowd. Yaya looked about her, there was a small girl on either side of her who she felt that in another life she was familiar with but couldn't quite place.

'I am Lea' said the one on her left,

'And me…... I am Anna.'

Lea proffered Yaya a piece of sausage but just as she was about to take it a large seagull with a frightening screech swooped down and grabbed it.

Yaya screamed, she hated seagulls after they had taken all her chips on Weymouth Beach, but this was not cold old England. This was Sicily…. and in front of her were soldiers fighting…… leaving their blood on the sand.

"Gladiators." Said Anna knowingly.

Yaya felt sick.

Chapter 20

Sanctuary

Amelie survived the fall thanks to Gabriel but was not as lucky as Yaya.

Even archangels get rushed, troubled and occasionally make mistakes as you already know. Just like the rest of us.

She woke to find herself on top of a strange pointed little hill amongst some pine trees. Gabriel pointed to the village and the Church below...... kissed her on the forehead...... and disappeared.

She was still dazed and could see that the hill was too steep to go straight down to the village and that she would have to backtrack. She was cheered to see that the village looked to be in her time. There were cars parked, and of a type she sort of recognised as recent. She looked along the obvious path to see a woman walking up towards her carrying some sort of bag. She was walking quickly, seemed to have seen her and was deliberately coming for her.

Amelie was relieved, reckoning that this was an ally sent by Gabriel to help her.

She suddenly became aware of a buzzing sound, and the lady's eyes met hers...... this sent a shiver down her spine…... they were a glowing bright yellow!

Her mouth went very dry, this was not a friend, but who was she?

Luka would have known who she was, well sort of. The Gladstone medical bag would have given her away. The friendly, family GP, married to the local vicar, who was a pillar of the community. A pretty dodgy pillar as it turned out.

The lady's sinuous, superior, exquisitely posh voice invaded her brain. Very 'far back' the English would describe that accent, more true than anyone realises.

'I am Ethelyn, Lord Chancellor to Catherine, queen of the Fomorians…… and you child are in league with my enemies.

My enemy's friend is my enemy I am afraid.

I have already met your ghastly cousin Luka and that senile old dotard who is your Grandfather. If you lot are the last hope of the Tuatha then they deserve their fate…... which is so surely rapidly approaching them.'

Amelie knew she had to be brave, and deep down believed Gabriel would in fact protect her.

She wasn't sure what to say so she straightened her back and stared defiantly into those evil eyes while remaining silent.

Ethelyn sort of flickered before her, as if not quite able to make her mind up whether to be a GP or an important Fairy.

The lack of fear and groveling seemed to upset her.

'Hmm, you're a spunky one and no mistake, but your day is about to get worse, a lot worse......like an ice cream, would you?'

Suddenly Amelie found herself in a car park, standing in front of an Ice Cream Van.

She could see the strange hill behind but had no recollection of walking down it. She shrugged inwardly, this was a world full of magic, just go with the flow.

The trouble with magic is that it can be black or white and she had a nasty feeling what sort this was.

A funny little man with a goatee beard was proffering her an ice cream cornet. She tried to stop herself, but she was hungry, tired, frightened and it seemed a small comfort in a troubled time.

She accepted the cornet, noted that the van was

decorated with autumn leaves and emblazoned in large letters MUNDI'S ICE CREAMS.

She went to lick the cream, for a second it tasted exquisite, the best she had ever had, and her spirits soared.

Then it all changed. The chocolate flake turned into an ugly fat worm and the exquisite taste became a mouthful of rotting slime, she tried to spit it out but if anything, it got worse.

She caught a glimpse of the van, what she had thought were autumn leaves were now obviously flames and Mr Mundi smiling wickedly at her discomfort looked positively devilish.

He laughed a deep unearthly unpleasant laugh that chilled her to the marrow. Grandad often tried a similar laugh but that was just funny and a bit naff, this was not: it was truly horrible.

She felt faint but she knew that to lose consciousness now would mean she might not ever wake up again.

 In that instant she knew anger was her best response, she fumed…. Quickly worked herself into a total tantrum and with surprising force threw the cornet straight back at Mr Mundi, scoring a direct hit…... stopping his evil laughter instantly……

horrible slimy ice cream messing up his neat beard…... As he flapped about the worm slipped into his mouth……. he tried to grab it but…... in his panic and flapping about ……. he swallowed it!

His eyes popped out, and for a delicious moment he had an expression of absolute horror and disgust.

'Not used to spirited young ladies fighting back' thought Amelie with a sense of triumph. For a moment she knew how St George must have felt, and the Dragon for that matter.

Running seemed like a good plan, so she did, and in the direction of the Church. She was half surprised that no one caught up and stopped her.

It was of course the same church that Luka and Grandad had been into. In fact, only a few minutes before, but she was not to know that.

It was open, the vicar had unlocked it as soon as he was sure Luka had truly gone, but she, in fear of being pursued, pulled the big door shut behind her. She turned the heavy large key, pulled it out, and placed it on the bookcase nearby.

Now feeling safer, she turned to look round the church, only to be confronted (it made her jump) by an anxious, curious, vicar asking why she had just locked the door?

Amelie of course did not know what to say.

Her story was just too fantastic for words, so she was effectively struck dumb.

The vicar was not a vicar for nothing, he spotted the distress and had already had one strange encounter. He wondered if they were related. Of course, they were! He told himself, having lived too long to believe in peculiar coincidences.

'Do you know Luka?'

Amelie was rocked back on her heels, suddenly seeing the vicar in an entirely new light. A man she could probably trust or at the very least someone who might understand.

'He is my cousin.'

With that very short exchange they both knew that they were involved in very mysterious events, probably beyond each one's understanding. Something the vicar was more used to than Amelie.

'I am Forster Holmes; vicar of this church and I will do my best to protect you from whatever it is that you are afraid of.'

'I am Amelie from Australia, and I am in a fantastic adventure that makes no sense. I have seen giants, been helped by an angel, met King Arthur and am now being chased by a frightening and seemingly important Fairie. Oh yes, and a very, very, nasty ice cream man. You might be able to help there...... because I think he is the Devil!'

The vicar could feel one of his migraines coming on.

He wondered briefly if the poor child was ill, with a psychotic delusional illness, but she didn't seem mad.

His previous experience suggested there was at least a grain of truth is her story. A loud banging on the church door curtailed any further musings on the truth.

'Forster, Forster open the flipping door! Have you got that ghastly girl in there? I need to see her.'

Amelie recognised the voice.'

'That is her, it is!! She is Ethelyn, Lord Chancellor of the Formorians, she is in league with that horrible little man.......'

The vicar slumped on a pew and stared past Amelie with empty despairing eyes, shaking his head.

'She is my wife.'

He almost whispered.

'She is a caring family GP, she is, she really is......'

But the doubts he had had for years were welling up inside him.

The banging on the door became more insistent.

The vicar suddenly seemed to decide, he jumped up and took hold of Amelie's hand.

'Come with me, I fear you are in danger little one.'

He led her to a narrow little alcove with a locked wrought iron gate, opening it with a key attached to his waste. As soon as Amelie was inside, he locked it behind them. There was a narrow spiraling descending flight of well-worn stone stairs that he shooed her down. She needed no encouragement despite that she was running down into the dark.

It seemed a long way down for a crypt in a little country church……. more than two hundred steps later they reached the bottom.

The vicar produced a torch, searched around, and alighted on a small trapdoor. They both pulled on a central ring and after some effort it began to move. With a strange creak and grating noise, it opened upwards and a strange head with long ears appeared squinting to avoid the worst of the torch beam.

'It is getting' flipping busy around here.'

Said Liplop mainly to himself. Cunningly managing to be in two places at once.

Of course, it was not actually Liplop but his brother…. but let's face it…… to us humans one big talking hare looks much like another.

Amelie wanted to hug the big hare, but Liplop's brother retreated in fright. He was a very English hare…... hugging was not for him.

The vicar started to whisper so loudly that in the confines of the crypt he was almost shouting.

'Er my friend, Amelie here, who I believe you know, is in some trouble with the Trickster and his band, I think she needs your special sort of help.'

'At your service vicar!'

He sort of chortled at his own feeble joke, and getting no reaction he went on,

'Mundi and his bunch are a rum and nasty lot, mind you your Missus is in it up to her neck……'

The vicar looked so crestfallen that the magical hare decided not to press charges.

'Come with me girl, it might be a bit rough, we have go to get through enemy lines as it were before we can even think of getting you home.'

He ushered Amelie through the trapdoor and down the set of stairs. Just as he was about to disappear there was a loud formidable female voice calling down.

'Forster, Forster get up here and bring that ghastly girl with you.'

'I don't fancy your supper tonight mate.'

Said the hare.

'I expect you will find it on the ceiling. See you....'

And disappeared.

The vicar sighed, shook his head, let the stone fall back into place and slowly retraced his steps preparing himself to face the music.

Chapter 21

Amelie meets a Leprechaun.

It wasn't as dark as she expected. There was some sort of light in the ceiling, no obvious bulbs she could see but glowing a faint red.

Liplop (let's call him that, it is a lot simpler, as his real name was Fortescue Magnificus Bumbletummer, known as Bumble bum for short, BB to his friends) ...... anticipated her question.

'Formorian quantums, that the lights'

He offered as an explanation that made no sense at all to Amelie.

'Be very quiet, we are underneath that hill, it's a rabbit warren it is...... and I don't get on with them. Be warned this is an evil place.'

At just that moment a root like thing sprang out of the wall and wrapped itself round Amelie's ankle. She squealed and fell; the ground was earthy and strangely unpleasant. The hare grabbed the root and bit through it with his enormous incisors in one easy motion.

'Come on, they've clocked us quicker than I hoped, this might get a little rough my girl.'

Suddenly the tunnel opened and there were three

possible routes. BB paused to consider.

'Wish you were called Ariadne, we need her ball of string, last thing we want is a face to face with a Minotaur'......

He saw Amelie looking blank and a bit frightened.

'You know story of Theseus and the ball of string and all that, Greek Myth......'

Amelie had some very dim recollection but just wanted to get out of here. Suddenly there was a roaring snuffling sound from the nearest entrance, it sounded like a cross bull!

'It's my fault.... their evil magic...... when you think of something nasty you conjure it up...... so that really is a Minotaur down that one...... half bull half man. And neither bit is happy....'

Amelie tried not to think of anything evil, but we all know that when you consciously try to stop thinking about something, you can't. So, she could not prevent a cackling black coated Witch from coming into her mind. Who instantly came a screaming and cackling from the second tunnel. Without the necessity of further thought they bolted down the third entrance.

There was no light in this one, which Amelie thought was probably good. It meant it wasn't commonly used and did not merit being lit. This was bad at the same time...... as they could not see where they were going.

BB was better at moving in the dark and offered his paw as the guide.

It smelt musty, earthy, but not really bad.

The hare was not hanging about.

Amelie nearly stumbled a few times, but he steadied her without dropping his pace. Soon she was getting out of breath, but he did not slacken. Just as she thought she could not go any further there was a faint light ahead.

It was daylight.... well sort of...... it was underground daylight. They emerged from the tunnel as if from a cave to find themselves in a great dome, so big as to almost feel as if they were in the open air, but they were not.

BB looked around, sniffed, and smiled as much as a magical hare can.

"This is Tuatha territory if I am not mistaken, we are not safe yet but a lot safer than we were."

Ahead lay open fields, slightly odd trees, a few scattered cottages, and all bathed this strange slightly misty light.

Amelie got her breath back and started to relax. At that moment she was grabbed from behind and pulled back into the tunnel. Her screams were smothered by a bag pulled over her head and all went black.

In her panic she was not sure, but she thought she heard Liplop (to her) cry out, scuffle and yell.

"I'll be back, I will!"

But she wondered if she had imagined it.

She felt herself being bound and carried like a trussed chicken. There was the chattering of small ugly voices, but she could not make out what was being said. Then something hit her on the head, and it all went black.

She woke to a loud insistent knocking. Finding herself in a whitewashed and spotless tiny little bedroom, unable at that moment recollect how she had got there. The knocking became more persistent.

Her head was still hurting, with a nasty soft painful bump but still she got up to explore ...... finding herself in a ranch like place. A little farmhouse in a wide-open space surrounded by countryside. Very odd countryside...... in that each time she looked away......when she looked back....... it had changed.

The knocking got more urgent; she found the door at last.

'Ok, ok, I am coming. Keep your hair on.'

Opening the door to find a little man staring up at her. A really little man, only about two foot tall and nearly as wide. He obviously liked red. Having a red floppy hat, a red jacket with gold buttons and very tight trousers that looked to Amelie in imminent danger of splitting disastrously. The large wide belt being the only object saving him from social disaster.

'Are you a dwarf?'

'How rude! Are you Snow poodling White?'

'Well, no......I am Amelie, and I am not entirely sure where I am.'

'Well, you are here, where else can you be?'

She understood the logic but not the meaning and couldn't immediately think of anything to say.

'Well, my name is Lep R Corn.' said the little fella cheerily.

'Oh, come on, you must be able to do better than that. Leprechauns are Irish mythical creatures only found in fairy stories.'

'Well clever clogs. If I am not very much mistaken that is precisely where you find yourself.'

'Anyway' said Amelie vaguely irritated.

'You can't be a Leprechaun; they wear green not red.'

'Is that so!' retorted the increasingly Irish little man.

'I could be a Luricawn, in fact it is that that I am, famous for me red britches am I.'

'They are too tight, if you bend over, they will split. You should lose some weight.'

'Well now, tis a fine state of affairs when someone youse hardly knows starts insulting you at the first opportunity. A proper prissy miss perfect you are. I can see tis to be a prickly start, and here is me only banging to tell you that your breakfast of pancakes, waffles, and marshmallows was getting cold.'

Amelie realised she was famished and accepted the offer immediately. It was indeed a very good if very sweet breakfast. The Luricawn was very attentive and fussed over her, bringing more and more waffles.

'Enough, enough. Thank you very much but that is enough, I am full to bursting.'

'T'will be me you'll be lookin' like soon.'

Amelie really hoped not.

'I don't believe you have told me your proper name, you were kidding me last time, weren't you?'

The little chap shuffled in a slightly bashful and embarrassed way and said almost under his breath.

'Spud.'

'What was that…. Pud? Is that right?'

'Spud'. He said a little more loudly.

'Spud! Is that it?'

'And why shouldn't it be.' He said pugnaciously.

'Short, well-rounded and not very pretty just like me self.'

'Why did you hit me on the head?'

Asked Amelie feeling they were just about on enough speaking terms to be able to ask the question.

'Ah…. that….'

He was obviously uncomfortable.

'Well, 'twas an accident it was, in the rush to get you away from them unfriendly fairies we banged your head in the tunnel.'

He looked a bit sheepish.

'Well, I'm sorry but twas in your best interests, it was it was.'

'But I was safe, Liplop was looking after me.'

'Oh yes, that talking bunny you mean? Well, he couldn't keep you safe from an angry mushroom. Means well I'll grant you, was doin' his best like I know but them Fairies would have had you the minute you were in the open, and then where would you be?'

Amelie had no idea, rubbed her bump and stared out at the strange landscape.

'So according to you, you rescued me.'

'That we did.'

'Who is we?'

'The DDs'

'What does that stand for?'

'The diminutive diggers.'

Amelie spotted a problem; Spud and his kind were obviously a race of little people and in other times might have been called dwarves. But this was obviously not how they saw themselves, and she was sensitive enough to pick up on this message.

'So where are the other.... DDs?'

'About, they are, about.'

He said by way of not saying anything.

'Now tis enuff, we need to get you settled.'

Amelie wondered if she should be going somewhere, wasn't there some sort of errand or quest she was supposed to be carrying out? It was all a bit hazy in her mind, she wondered aloud if she should be doing something?

'What is it that you like to be doing?' asked Spud.

'Well, I like, horse riding, painting sometimes and well doing things with my friends.... I would like my phone back too.'

'No phones here but …. right then some paints and canvasses it is then, and I will get old Glastyn over, he might give you a ride if 'n he's in a good mood.'

'Have you seen Esme and Yaya?'

'Can't say that I have, and who might they be?'

'My sister and my cousin, we came here together but I seem to have lost them. Perhaps I should be going home?'

'Well, you're not goin' anywheres till her Ladyship says so, an' she's not here to ask. Don't expect her for a while.'

Amelie was not as distressed as you would have expected her to be, remaining in a dreamy sort of state.

'Her Ladyship?' she queried without in fact being very interested.

'The Queen of Middle Kingdom, she is a Goddess in fact…… well she certainly thinks she is……. Lady Danu…... she is the boss round here. She knows you are here and will use you when she is good an' ready. But neither you, me or the fates know when that might be.'

As if by magic, in all probability it was by magic, brushes, paints, an easel, and a stack of lily-white canvasses appeared. So, it was the most natural thing in the world to just start painting.

The thing about painting is you must concentrate, to get a picture of what you are going create an image of in your head. Then you have to draw the outline on the canvas, and finally to fill in the detail.

It is not easy, and to most people it is hard to do. Children are naturally better painters than most grownups and Amelie found she had a talent undreamed of at her home in Perth.

She began to paint the landscape she saw; she managed a canvas a day and when she had ten, she laid them all out on the ground to see them in sequence.

Magic!

Chapter 22

A Special Horse.

The paintings were so very different, yet she had painted from the same spot every day. The landscapes were fantastical, intricate, mysterious and oh so colourful. They were all quietly busy she thought, or were they busily quiet, or was that the same thing? She sort of recognised them in a dim ill-defined sort of way.

'Spud I don't really understand what is happening to me, I paint the same thing every day, but it is never the same, I think I might have seen these landscapes somewhere else before, but I can't think where?'

The little man replied but he was changing in front of her, this was a warm embracing educated voice, not at all the Irish trickster.

'Under the Earth I go; on the oak leaf I stand. I ride on the filly that was never foaled, and I carry the lost in my hand.

Once it was where it was not, beyond seven times seven countries and the Sea of Operencia, behind an old stove in a crack in the wall in the skirt of an old witch and there in the seven times seventh fold...a white flea.... and in the middle of its back the beautiful city of a Queen.'

This was very strange, reality was drifting away, like her paintings. For a moment Amelie wondered if she had died and began to cry. It was all so unreal and yet at the same time so vivid. She felt a little hand take hers.

'And in that city beyond all time space and being were so fantastical no living being could comprehend. Ineffable. There was just the light of the light that passes all understanding with the joy of the knowledge of the knowledge.'

She realised that this was a good voice, one that covered you and reassured even if she did not understand anything it said, the fear lessened.

'I see this place is not for you little one. You love horses do you not. Mine is called Glastyn, come he will carry you free.'

And a new Spud, taller, thinner, almost handsome, pushed her up onto a horse she did not know was there.

And what an animal! Whiter than white, his perfectly balanced proportions increased his beauty, but he was more than that.

Amelie knew horses, her own called Rooster was

magnificent, but not like this! This creature was greater than the sum of its parts, a perfection, magical, powerful and she knew immediately that this steed was far, far cleverer than she could ever be. He belonged to the Gods, and she knew it.

Spud climbed on behind exhibiting a skill he had hidden well till now.

They rode on Glastyn the horse for miles, or was it days?

When she thought about it later, she could remember the journey only in the sense that they travelled from one strange dark place to another lighter place.

There were images in her head of rivers… valleys… caves…. Mountains… deserts…. stone circles …. strange pyramids…. but they were just that…. isolated images…. without the coherence of a definite route to and from point A to point B.

At last, Glastyn stopped its wondrous gallop. It was light, in a twinkly flickery torch lit sort of way it was clear they were in a cave…. but no ordinary cave.

There were columns, that Amelie could see were stalagmites or was it stalactites, she could never remember which came from the top or the bottom. (t=top)

Spud helped her down and pointed to a little chair that seemed to be part of the stone. She sat down and was surprised how soft and warm it felt to the touch; immediately she realised how exhausted she was and fell into a deep dreamless sleep.

When she awoke, she was lying on a soft bed with what seemed like a vivid painting of the Milky Way on the ceiling. Then she started laughing to herself as she remembered her favourite joke.

...... Sherlock Holmes and Dr Watson went on a camping trip. After a good meal and a bottle of red, they lay down for the night and went to sleep. Some hours later Holmes woke up, nudged his faithful friend, and said,

"Watson, I want you to look up at the sky and tell me what you see."

Watson said, "I see millions and millions of stars."

Sherlock said, "And what does that tell you?"

After a minute or so of pondering Watson said,

"Astronomically, it tells me that there are millions of galaxies and potentially billions of planets. Astrologically, I observe that Saturn is in Leo. Horologically, I deduce that the time is approximately a quarter past three in the morning. Theologically, I can see that God is all powerful and that we are small and insignificant. Metereologically, I suspect that we will have a beautiful day today. What does it tell you?"

Holmes was silent for about 30 seconds and said,

"Watson, you idiot! Someone has stolen our tent!"…….

'I am glad to hear you laughing, tinkling diamonds in what could be sea of sorrow.' Said Spud

'Not all that experience the true darkness of evil recover so well. The universe has wonderful restorative powers.'

She began to remember. She knew the landscapes now, they were Judy's pastels, but the dark things that had happened…. She shuddered….

'Thank you, I am not sure what for exactly or… well I am not really sure about anything, but I think you rescued me from something pretty ghastly… though I don't know what happens now…Do you tell stories, Spud?'

'No, not me but I do weave tales like the one you are in now. It is not my story for the telling, but it is yours for the living.'

Amelie was puzzled, it sort of made sense, but it didn't.

'So, let me get this straight, you are making what is happening to me, happen.'

'In a way, but not how you suppose, the dice are rolled, the cards are dealt, the wheel of fortune spins, and I will jump the universe.'

'Spud you make no sense at all.'

'Perhaps the world you live in makes no sense.'

'Of course, it does.'

'Are you so sure?'

Amelie, forced to think about something she had always taken for granted, thought she was sure, it was so obvious, but what was happening made no sense and she was still alive so…. there must be an explanation but what was it? She picked on a phrase...

'Jump the universe, that is like a nursery rhyme, cows over moons, do you mean what you say or are you just trying to keep me guessing?'

'You may think as you like but you can jump universes with me, there is no difficulty choosing.'

'Surely there is only one universe, the one we are living in?'

Spud began to alter, was he smiling?

He began to flicker and break into patterns of light, changing into fragmented geometric shapes...... splitting into parts...... each of which was a reduced-size copy of the whole of him.

The effect was breathtakingly beautiful, but Amelie found her senses being stretched by the sheer complexity of what she was witnessing.

It was chaotic but ordered in a repetitive way, everywhere she looked was breaking up into myriads of smaller replicas of what had been there.

She could still sort of see him or his constituent parts, but even that was changing. Now she could see stars, galaxies oh so many, she was amongst them, she was part of them, she was a million, million, universes, and she was not afraid.

There was a sort of flash and suddenly she was back to reality or at least what passed for it. Spud was definitely smiling.

'So now you know.'

Amelie was not at all certain of what she did know, except that she wanted some certainty. A sense of insignificance flowed into her, she wanted this dream or whatever it was to end now.

'Can you take me home Spud, or at least back where I started?'

Chapter 23

Esme meets someone special.

The image of Poundbury began to fade, but the valley below the Glastonbury Tor was filled with a thick fog.

Esme's heart was still pounding, she was fearful and distressed at the fall of Amelie and Yaya. Morgana took her hand and instantly her spirits lifted, no words were spoken but she knew that the girls had survived somehow. Suddenly the great and shining Arthur towered above her.

'You Esme are part of this unravelling, and your part is set, and important part it is.'

He gestured and the dragonfly moved beside him. Arthur lifted her without ado onto Meg's back, Morgana helped strap her in.

'To Ringsted Round.'

She whispered and Meg took off.

Esme's mind was buzzing, so much had happened, and yet she seemed no nearer to knowing what her role in this strange mystery was.

All was mist below her, suddenly there was a break in the murk, and she saw the sea. It was grey, unfriendly, not at all like the sea she was used to in

Australia. The dragonfly hovered over a little bay, there was nothing there…. then something very strange happened…. the bay began rapidly changing as she looked. She couldn't work it out at first but then she remembered that sequence in an old film she had once watched…... The Time Machine.

She knew now with absolute certainty that time was unravelling. She assumed they were going forward but realised it was equally likely to be going backwards. Dwellings appeared and disappeared…. there were forests and then none…. the shoreline changed shape…. it was dizzying.

She felt a bump as if Meg had passed through a barrier, and they came into land on a little shingly beach. It was not cold, but for an Aussie it wasn't warm either.

It seemed deserted. She was still holding the little sword, which seemed to have lost the magic, it was rusty now and had no edge. Still, she kept hold of it though thinking it might yet be important and even if not, it would be a memento, an anchor to the story in her mind.

Unstrapped, she slid from the dragonfly landing on the stony beach. With a whizz Meg took off and vanished.

She was alone with her sword, the sea was still grey and a bit rough, and the seagulls circling overhead were screaming.

A voice behind her said.

'The souls of drowned sailors my Aunt told me.'

She wheeled round quickly to see a young boy, about 11 she thought, in old fashioned clothes standing close by. He smiled and misunderstood her surprise.

'The seabirds you know. They always sound so sad and desperate.'

He paused to study her. Esme was wearing jeans and a modern jacket top, and brandishing a little rusty sword, well more a big dagger really. Not surprisingly he seemed troubled. He wrinkled his brow and seemed to be struggling to get more words out. He almost looked like his own description of the haunting Herring Gull cry.

Esme understood immediately, later she was unable to say how, but she knew immediately who this was.

'I am not her.' She said.

'Then who are you?'

'I am Esme, and I am here for a reason, but I don't

know what it is.'

'You speak in riddles……I come here every day I can hoping to find a sign.'

The waves crackled on the shingle, sucking at the pebbles as they retreated.

'I wonder if I might be a sort of sign?'

He stared at her and slowly shook his head.

'No, you are…...well…. too flesh and blood…not like her…...'

'You mean I am not a Fairie.'

His eyes bored deep into her soul, seeking for some knowledge, nor knowing how to respond then she recited.

'It was many and many a year ago.

In a kingdom by the sea

That a maiden there lived who you may know

By the name of Annabel Lee.'

'You know her, you really know her! She was here day after day, she called herself Belli, but her real name was Annebeline.'

He looked desperate.

'I must see her again; her laugh was the greatest noise in the whole world…. can you take me to her?'

'No Edgar, I can't but something must happen, we are here for a reason, but neither of us know what it is.'

The young boy shook his head in a confused sort of way, how did this strange girl in even stranger clothes seem to know him? And that poem she spoke, well it was in his head too. This was more magic, ever since he had met Belli life had become weird.

Esme shivered involuntarily.

'We can't stay on the beach forever, it is cold. Do you know what month it is? Feels like March. Perhaps I could go home with you?'

'You don't know the month! Just who or what are you? And why do you have a rusty fire poker?'

For the first time she could hear the American twang in the voice, she smiled.

'Sword, it is a proper sword but er, well I think all this is a bit complicated, it might take some time to explain, can we just go somewhere warm.'

A young woman in very old-fashioned long dress

and tatty shawl appeared on the shingle, carrying what appeared to be a lump of clay. She spotted them and smiled.

'Come here you young uns and see something real old.' Her accent was deepest Dorset but very pleasant. She laid the clay down on the beach. It was a big fish head fossil. Esme stared at it.

'That's an Ichthyosaur skull. Wow what a specimen.'

'Howm yer knowz that? A mean what is it you called it?'

'Ichthyosaur, well I just recognise it, seen it in museums'......she paused and looked at her.

'Oh dear, I think I know who you are as well. You are Mary, aren't you?'

'Yes, I be Mary Anning from Lyme, you knows moi name. I dinna realize I was that famous.'

Esme was confused, she knew to say more would just confuse everyone, so she just smiled and nodded. Edgar was studying the fossil.

'Wow, must be before the flood.'

'Oi got larts of them, we got a shop you know, you should come if'n yer ever in Lyme.'

She picked up the clay embedded skull.

'Sorry got to go, my brother will along with the cart.'

And she disappeared down the lane.

Esme was still cold and Edgar even more suspicious. He hesitated, decided to trust her after all as a potential friend, and led her off the beach to where a small pony was tied.

'Can you ride?'

She nodded and soon they were both on the pony's back and plodding into the low hills behind the beach. It was hard to talk on horseback, especially as she had difficulty pushing the sword through her belt without stabbing herself, so they lapsed into silence and after an hour or so came into a small village with a wide main street.

"Maine."

Said Edgar as they clopped along the cobbles. The road narrowed and they had to squeeze past a little thatched hovel because a cart full of evil smelling dung was obstructing the carriageway.

Then they heard a commotion behind them, shouting, a horse galloping across the cobbles, then a shot. As they moved past the smelly cart a big man on an even bigger horse hurtled towards them, shouting for them to get out of his way. He squeezed through the gap…. overturning the cart in the process and effectively blocking the road to his pursuers. For pursuers they were.

A group of men dismounted quickly…… seeing they had muskets the children jumped off the pony and pulled him behind the hovel wall. A volley rang out, but the horseman was a fair way away by now and they missed. He disappeared into a small copse and was gone.

'Blarsted Bill Watch! We'll get him one day lads.'

There was much mumbling and grumbling and the men packed up and went back into the village.

'Who is Bill Watch?'

Whispered Esme.

'A famous highwayman in these parts.'

Seeing her blank stare, he went on.

'An armed robber who holds up the stagecoaches, the ones that run from Shaftesbury to Weymouth, I think. My uncle says he has been doing it for years, but they never seem to catch him. He reckons he is a phantasm.'

'Well, he seemed pretty real just now.'

Edgar smiled a conspiratorial sort of smile.

'Actually, he is a friend of mine, well more a relative

really, cousin or something and he is meant to be taking me back to London, soon, I think. So, in a way I hope they both don't and do catch him.'

This made no sense to Esme who changed the subject.

'Er, I wonder what year this is?'

'You are strange one I'll be bound, look it is April 4th, 1820, if that is all right with you. Oh yes, and it is a Tuesday.'

He hesitated, and more to humour her than meaning the question seriously, asked.

'And what time is it where you are from?'

Esme was not sure whether to tell the truth or to lie, it was all too unbelievable, she decided it was probably better just to tell the truth.

'Well, I don't know what day it is because I have been away, but I think it is August 2023.'

He just stared, jaw dropping slightly open, so she went on.

'With my sister and cousins, we have sort of got involved in a real fairy story, only it has got very complicated, and I don't know what is to come.

I have lost all the others and have no idea what is

going to happen to me which is funny really because I know what is going happen to you.'

As soon as the words were out of her mouth, she knew she should not have said them.

'You know me?'

Esme's 'oops oh dear look' spread all over her face. She tried shaking her head, not even convincing herself, so she looked at her shoes.

'Well, what is my full name...eh? go on then.'

She had got this far and that seemed reasonable to tell him.

'Edgar Allan Poe'

'I don't like the Allan.'

'Well, you had better get used to it because when you are famous that is what everyone calls you.'

Suddenly he was angry,

'You are a witch, a teller of lies, I don't want you near me......

He grabbed the pony and mounted quickly and started off up the hill.

Esme was terrified to be on her own, in the wrong time and no way out. Tears welled up and with a tiny breaking voice she called after him.

'Don't go, please don't go. Please, please help me. Take me with you, I am not a witch, I am not, just a girl in the wrong place and the wrong time.'

Edgar stopped the pony and sat still. Esme caught up, he looked down at her, smiled a wan smile, shrugged, held out his hand, she clambered on and off they went heading towards the small clump of trees that Bill Watch had disappeared into.

The wood was damp, very quiet and a bit spooky. She was nervous, afraid Big Bad Bill would jump out, afraid Edgar would leave her and afraid of what the future held.

There was a rustling, scatting, sort of sound that made her jump. Edgar laughed and pointed, there was a bushy tailed red squirrel nibbling an acorn while keeping a weather eye on them. She relaxed a little, and soon they were in the open again, from the top of the hill they could see the spires of a sizeable town.

'Dorchester.'

Said Edgar quietly.

Esme strained hard to get her bearings, it took her a while but as she made out the shape of Maiden Castle to her left, she looked across the valley and could clearly make out the Poundbury Hill Fort.

'Well Witch can you recognise where you are?'

She pointed.

'That is Maiden Castle and on the other side is Poundbury Hill Fort, it is near there that my adventure began.'

He looked puzzled.

'I can nearly understand you, what did you call that earthwork?'

'Maiden Castle.'

He nodded to himself,

'And the other one?'

'Poundbury hill fort.'

He screwed up his eyes and nodded to himself. After a while he said almost to himself,

'Maidun Hill and Pummery Castle, same but different…… I stay in Pummery Grange near the old walls. T'is there we are bound…….'

Then he tried to add as a casual remark but they both knew it wasn't.

'So, I am to be famous, for what I pray?'

Esme knew she was in difficult and dangerous territory, so she did not reply immediately…. eventually she said.

'I don't think I can really tell you; it will upset…. well things…. but you will make your mark on the world…. gosh I feel like a Gipsy lady giving out fortunes. I can see why you call me a witch, but I am not, honestly. I am just an ordinary girl out of her time in a very strange adventure.'

Nothing was said for what seemed like an age then, at last, Esme spoke.

'Tell me about Annabel Lee.'

Chapter 24

Luka meets the Teddy Bears

Luka was fed up. He had been excited by the idea of a bulldozer rushing round the houses bulldozing things, but nothing had happened...... and it was hours since Grandad and Sir Mortimer had gone to find one.

He knew he should be part of the adventure. The Goddess Danu herself had told him, and those images were still flashing through his mind. The truth was he was bored, as well as frustrated, and sneaked out without telling anyone.

He walked past the Tutankhamun museum, thought about going in, but those Egyptian mummies, wrapped up in bandages for thousands of years freaked him out.... though he wouldn't admit that to anyone.

He was heading for the river and as he came near the bottom of the town, he saw the Teddy Bear Museum. He shivered and remembered...... we all have strange inexplicable dislikes and in Luka's case it was teddy bears.... he thought them creepy.... weird, and well...... frightening. To him this museum as a young child was the worst experience of his life.

'Give me Mummies any day' he thought to himself.

He was about to hurry on when the large teddy bear outside waved at him. He stopped to see if it was just a mechanical device and went to get a closer look. The bear smiled a crooked not quite right smile, lopsided and a little unsettling. He knew instantly that this was all part of the strange goings on. It was very tempting just to run, and he even tried to, but the message he sent to his legs failed. The bear's smile became smug in a deeply unpleasant sort of way, and strange forces pulled him inside. There he found a full human size girl bear, wearing a Victorian servant's outfit who curtsied politely and pointed with trembling paw up the very narrow winding stairs.

Up he went because it was his fate to do so. Finding himself in a very strange room that he half remembered. There were several large bears in full old fashioned dress, but this was a different room from the last time he was there. Now his worst nightmare had come true, they were alive! They all turned to look at him with penetrating doll's glass eyes. The room was full of a cloying tobacco smoke with an underlying smell of old people and damp walls. He was trapped and wanted to scream!

A big old bear with a huge Meerschaum pipe just like…. Well…... you know who…... turned to stare at him. He seemed perplexed and looked for assistance at a large lady bear in a fine old blue dress. She raised her chin and looked very haughty.

'She looks like a galleon in full sale, eh my boy?'

Said Mr Pipe in a surprisingly friendly and bearish sort of voice. Luka was not sure if he was meant to reply, but the inner scream was fading.

'Cat got your tongue. Come, come youngster, it is rude not to reply to your elders. Who are you I pray?'

'Er......well I am Luka, I come from Split in Croatia, but I am staying with my grandparents and have got involved in a weird adventure and I think you are part of it.'

'Hmmm, I had not realised I was part of an adventure, how exciting.'

He took a huge pull on his enormous pipe and exhaled. The room went dark with a cloying sweet-smelling smoke.

'I do wish you would put that ghastly smelly pipe down Ebenezer, choking us all you are. And you boy, well you can't walk in here and expect to have tea just like that. I mean it is an obligation, not a right……. Fenella, I suppose you must make some tea, buttered crumpets, marmalade jam and clotted cream should do. Use the best tea pot, we don't wish to look shabby do we…?'

Fenella, a thin nervous looking bear in a maids outfit, who had greeted him initially looked hesitant.

'Well DO WE?'

Said mother bear in an extremely upper-class voice.

The maid scuttled out, and there was a lot of crashing, banging, hissing, and clanking sounds from behind the door.

Luka stood still, unsure of what to say or do…. echoes of the Mad Hatter's tea party floated through his mind…. he even wondered if all this was a creation of his own imagination. No fool this boy.

Looking around the room made it crystal clear that all was not in prime condition. The walls that had once been white were now tobacco stained yellow and peeling. The furniture was very definitely past its best, stained, torn, scuffed, and a bit wonky too.

There was a Times newspaper lying where Ebenezer had laid it down, Luka strained to see the date. 1V-1V- MDCCCXX.

They had done Roman numerals at school, but he had not paid proper attention and he was struggling to work it out. He knew it was 4th of the 4th but he was unsure of the other date. He shook himself to concentrate. M that was a thousand, D he thought was 500 and C well that was a hundred, like Centurion, wasn't it? So, 3 Cs would make 300. The sum was 1000+500+300= 1800. X was ten, he was sure of that, but the sum must be wrong. 1820 was impossible, just outside the door it was 2022.

But it was a Teddy Bear Museum...... so perhaps it was just a copy of an old paper...... set in a room that was a copy of an old room. Yes, that was the most likely answer in a situation for which there was no obvious rational explanation. He smiled inwardly at his own deductive abilities.

Nothing seemed to have happened while he had

been concentrating, it was as if only him interacting with the bear tableaux brought them to life. He looked at Mrs Bear meaning to ask a question about the date. This seemed to wake her as she suddenly exclaimed in a cross sort of way,

'Oh, where is that foolish girl, she is taking an age, you would think she was making the marmalade. Fenella….!'

She yelled.

'Get a move on, our guest is famished and will fade away with starvation if you take much longer….'

Turning to Luka

'You are famished aren't you, my boy?'

He wasn't, but he nodded politely because it seemed the right thing to do.

The door burst open. Fenella wheeled in a very rickety contraption covered in crumpets, teacups, large flowery China tea pot, and jars of jam…. plus a huge bowl of cream.

It wobbled, clicked, threatened to lose a wheel but eventually the trolley was stationary in the middle of the room. Mrs Bear took on the role of tea mistress.

She piled up a small tea plate with buttered crumpets and handed it to Luka.

'Help yourself to all the goodies young man… help you grow big and strong.'

Ebenezer dived in without any of the manners Luka had been taught. Immediately he began ladling very hot crumpets with impossible amounts of marmalade and cream on them. Then stuffing them into his mouth with no ceremony at all, despite them being far too hot to eat.

Luka was amused, posh Mrs Bear didn't seem to mind, so he helped himself too. They were cooler now and very nice they were too. He waited till his mouth was empty of crumpet to ask, as innocently as he could manage, what day it was.

Ebenezer, not as fussy, sprayed Luka with assorted crumpet and marmalade goblets as he spluttered loudly.

'Why today is Tuesday young man. All day it is Tuesday.'

'Yes Mr Ebenezer' he replied wiping his face clear of spittle with his sleeve.

'But what month and especially what year?'

'My you are an excessively ignorant boy; don't they teach you anything in school these days? It is April, April the fourth in the glorious reign of that fat preening Prinny, only two months on the throne but he has been there for years. Why tis 1820!'

Luka had feared as much… he took another crumpet to cheer himself up.

After he had eaten it, he became lost in his own thoughts, and just stared at the floor wondering what to do next. He knew what was happening made no sense, and thought that some of it was his own mind creating sort of hallucinations but was he really in the past?

Obviously talking Teddy Bears were not real, but then neither was Sir Mortimer and yet he was. He was friends with two Ghosts, well that was impossible too.

He shook his head and looked up.

The room was empty!

Chapter 25.

Old Dorchester

'I think Belli is a Fairy.... but she was even more.... she looked like my mother and at the same time looked like.... well, someone I could love forever....my mother died when I was too young to know her.... but I just know Annebeline was her spirit. She knew me, she really knew me, and now she has gone.'

'I think she might be an echo of someone who you are going to meet.' Esme said.

Edgar whipped around and fixed her with a manic stare.

'What do you know? In the name of Christ what do you know.'

Esme was afraid and felt tears welling up. Edgar continued staring at her.

'You know about me Witch! But you won't tell me, I am in confusion and despair.'

By now Esme was really crying. She could not think of anything to say that would not make it worse, so she tried to sob as quietly as she could.

She had remembered what she had learned from Wikipedia after reciting the poem. That Edgar married Virginia who was only 13, when he was 27 and that their relationship was strange, more brother and sister than man and wife, but that he had been inconsolable when she died, aged only 24. He had begun drinking too much and died far too young. She felt it was best to say nothing at all.

At last Edgar turned his head away, shook the reins, and the horse plodded on. Near a little river at the bottom of the town they came to a road and turned up what appeared to be a rather fine high street with imposing buildings stretching away up a gentle hill.

Esme began to almost recognise things; this was Dorchester.... in all its Eighteenth-Century glory.

A stagecoach brushed past them, shaking her out of her misery. The driver yelling for them to get out of the way, and then a young boy nearly ran into them too. Edgar shouted at him to look where he was going but he seemed lost in himself.

Then Esme nearly fell off the pony, she recognised him! 'Luka, Luka! It's me Esme, it's me.'

The boy stopped in the middle of the road. A horseman at full gallop, who looked a lot like the highwayman Bill Watch thought Esme, shouted for him to get out of the way. They could see a large group of riders, obviously in pursuit, coming towards them.

All this shouting woke Luka out of his dream. He grasped the reins and pulled them into the same little alleyway they had just emerged from, as the chasing pack thundered by.

He peered at her.

'That is you Esme isn't it…. well, am I glad to see you'. He looked at her companion.

'Who is this?'

'I can speak you know. I am Edgar and am I to presume you know this witch?'

'This is my cousin, and we are both in a weird adventure that is like living in a nightmare.'

A thought came to him.

'Esme, you know what day it is?'

'Tuesday April 4th, 1820, if I am not mistaken.'

The fact she knew rather took the wind out of his sails.

'Oh, you knew…. but I mean how are we going to get back?'

Esme had no immediate answer to that, but she felt instinctively that if they got up to near where the house was, something would happen. Not exactly a plan! so she decided just to shrug her shoulders.

'We are going to Edgar's English uncle's place.'

She looked for affirmation, but Edgar just looked away, obviously not a happy bunny.

Luka looked nervously behind him at the little house where he had just had the most bizarre tea with full size teddy bears. Deciding it was just too strange to relate he said nothing. Edgar gently started the pony with a dig of his heels, and they again set off up the high street. Luka walking beside them, taking more care this time.

The street was much shorter than Esme remembered, in a flash they were back in open country. She recognised the Poundbury hill fort off to their right and soon they were on top of the hill, where the grandparents now lived. She sighed.... they still seemed so far way.

Luka, who was good at landmarks, pointed at an impressive large old stone building that they were approaching.

'Look Esme, I think this Farm is where the modern Duchy farm building is. It is laid out in the same way, facing East.'

Esme looked and visions of Cavalon that had become Camelot, so long ago, filled her mind. For one so young she had seen so much.

'Arthur and Camelot.' She murmured to herself.

Edgar heard and looked perplexed.

'My uncle says this was Camelot, that King Arthur ruled here, that Merlin still lives here.'

'Who is Merlin?' asked Luka.

'You know,' said Esme.

'Arthur, knights of the round table, the sword Excalibur, Merlin the wizard….'

She released her sword and waved it for no other reason than that it seemed the right thing to do.

'Morgana Le Fay, the witch…' growled Edgar now dismounted and staring at Esme.

Luka did remember,

'Oh yes The Sword in the Stone, and my video game of Merlin and the Zombies.'

'Zombies? What are Zombies?' asked Edgar.

Luka was in his element.

'The undead, they climb out of graves and stuff and if they catch you, you become one of them. They eat flesh.'

'They are pretty silly if you ask me'. Interrupted Esme. 'They all stagger about and fall to bits, and they look awful.'

'You have seen them?'

'Yes of course.'

They both said at once, but then realised that Edgar would have no idea about films or TV. He was staring at them.

'And you were not scared out your wits? I have read that new story by a woman, Mary Shelley, about a monster made from the dead, by a Dr Frankenstein. It haunts my dreams, yet I feel for the poor creature.... created with no love.... this a Zombie, yes .... I see now.... But where....'

A different older voice rang out.

'Is that you Edgar, where have you been boy? I feared for you.'

A tall man emerged from the porch of the dilapidated farmhouse now directly in front of them. There was a huge black bird perched on his shoulder. Luka knew him at once and Esme recognised him as the man she had recited Annabel Lee to, around the kitchen table, very near where they were now.... but 200 years in the future.

They both felt a quite explicable surge of relief. They were now connected to their story and not

229

entirely lost. The familiar farmer stared at the children, and was there? Surely yes…a knowing smile.

Edgar had no idea.

'Er sorry Uncle, these are my friends I met. We sort of lost track of time.'

Esme nodded to herself, acknowledging the deeper truth of the remark.

Uncle, in his present incarnation, was Sir Mortimer Wheeler 'ish. He had an unkempt moustache and a wild head of hair, he was wearing a waistcoat, buttoned up shirt, sturdy tweed trousers and riding boots. Every inch a slightly eccentric Lord of the Manor.

'Quoth the Raven……' Blurted out Esme.

Uncle patted the bird.

'I have tried to teach him, but he just croaks….'

Then quite unmistakably the bird said.

'Nevermore.'

Luka, seeing the uncle's lips move a little, realised that this was just ventriloquy but the others, especially Edgar, were flabbergasted. Uncle laughed and the bird with lumbering flaps flew off into a nearby tree and glared down at them.

Esme walked a bit to the side of the farmhouse and found a long narrow zigzag crack in the stonework running from the apex of the roof to the large pond at the base. It really looked as if the house could collapse at any moment. She smiled to herself.

'I know your name 'Uncle' it is Roderick, and unless I am mistaken Usher, and your wife or sister is called Madeleine.'

Edgar's jaw dropped, he was amazed and almost angry. 'You are a witch, you really are.'

Luka felt he had to defend Esme,

'No, she is not, she just knows things because she reads a lot.'

Esme murmured.

'Yes, I have read The Fall of the House of Usher and I now know where the idea came from.'

Uncle Roderick put his finger to his lips in a 'be quiet' gesture, and Esme suddenly realised that she had some sort of responsibility to not let too many cats out of the bag. Roderick looked at her hard.

'I will have you know young lady that that crack has been there for at least two centuries so I feel we a have a little more time.'

Just a that moment there was a rumble in the ground and the earth shook. Roderick pushed the children away and there was a huge rending noise then a splashing, crumbling, falling sound. They watched in horror as the side of the big old house collapsed into the farmyard pond.

Roderick and Edgar ran towards the collapsing house, shouting.

'Madelaine' and 'Auntie' respectively.

Luckily before they could risk their lives in the debris a dusty tall white figure appeared in the twisted doorway and staggered out, Roderick caught her just as her legs gave way.

There was a sound of a galloping horse, Esme turned to see Bill Watch charging towards them, this time without obvious pursuers.

'Time to go young Edgar.'

The horseman shouted and scooped up the boy in one easy movement and put him in the saddle to his front. Edgar seemed resigned and seemed as if he had half expected what was happening.

'You will remember me Esme, won't you?'

She felt a great lump in her throat, found herself blowing a kiss, and they were gone.

Luka was tugging her hard.

'Look, look Esme, it is very strange.'

And it really was.

Chapter 26

The Great God Pan

Amelie was afraid, she found herself in another huge dark cave. Spud had disappeared. A few flickering torches illuminated the space, and what a space it was!

Massive stalactites (they hang from the top) and stalagmites (they grow upwards) were outlined by the flickering torchlight, creating strange effects, like the legs of trolls coming to eat you for their supper.

A stream nearby was running away from her.... that seemed the way to go. Heart pounding, the shadows playing with her mind, she walked and stumbled for what seemed like miles... then the walls began to change. She was still in a cave, but this was Lascaux, Altamira, and all the other Neolithic painted caves rolled into one, then multiplied by one hundred!

The chamber was bigger than an underground St Peter's Rome. Every inch was painted with images of long dead animals, mammoths, deer, elk, and huge cows (she later learned they were called Aurochs) and in front of her was a tableaux that seemed to light itself up as she stared at it. There were hundreds of stick men, some in strange costumes, a few seemed half man half animal, like centaurs, lizard men, and birds with arms not wings. Time slowed, there were pipes, faint…. but there.

The melody, all the time getting louder, gradually crept into the spaces filling her head. It was like those continuous pipe records played in Dentist's surgeries to stop you being terrified. This however was not a calming tune; it was a magical one.

Amelie thought of the Pied Piper of Hamlyn and squinted into the gloom to see who was playing. She would have to follow him…… she already knew that.

The rhythm began to speed up, the figures on the wall seemed to move, soon they were running, and the animals too. It was dizzying watching this amazing ancient chase. She fell backwards and turned to save herself by catching hold of what seemed like a post.

After a short while she experienced a creeping and terrifying realisation that this was not a post……it was a hairy bony leg. Holding on with both hands she slowly looked up……her heart was beating very fast. Above her was a huge half man…. half goat…. at least 3 metres tall…. playing the pipes.

He was satyr like…. cloven hoofed…. shaking Amelie free he began prancing with his pipes just touching his lips.

All the animals were racing around the cave. The stick men chasing them, and still the frenzy escalated. His eyes met hers, the power knocking her backward to the floor so that the stampede of the Deer, the Aurochs and Bison crashed across her vision, pounding a rhythm into her brain. Then he laughed.

She was expecting a horrible laugh, but it wasn't. It was gentle, embracing and knowing, he smiled too. A voice in her head asked,

'Do you know me?'

Amelie sort of did, an old memory or something.

'You are Pan, aren't you, The Horned….'

She paused for a beat realising the immensity of what she was about to say.

'…. The Horned God.'

He raised a sort of eyebrow in an amused congratulatory way and turned deeper into the cave. It was not dark anymore, Pan radiated a warmth that became light, and walls were full of racing images like one continuous tablet screen.

After a while Amelie realized they were going up. Soon there were little waterfalls, then bigger ones. Climbing should have been hard, but it was as if there was no gravity…. it was magic she told herself…. remembering being told that magic was only science you did not understand, but a voice in her head rebuked her.

'Magic is Magic.'

The images on the wall were changing, it was softer, and closer. The men were now real but with strange faces that seemed they were made with leaves and very green…... the animals had fleshed out…. now there were lions… boar… water buffalo…. even kangaroo!

And lots of big animals she did not recognise. Still, they went up…… time did not seem to matter here but Amelie was sure it was hours.

At the top of an especially dramatic waterfall, Pan stopped, turned, and offered her an apple. She hesitated, apples in fairy stories tend not to be good luck. The God cocked his head on one side with a good humoured quizzical look that reminded her of a favourite old dog back home. She took it gratefully, realising that she was, in fact, famished. Going for broke and taking a huge bite, she was overcome by joy and wonder.

It wasn't just the best apple she had ever tasted but the best anything. In fact, it was anything, whatever she thought of, it tasted of, but the best that taste could be. She went through fish and chips, hamburger, lobster, duck pancakes, ice cream, chocolates, and her favourite biscuits. By the time she finished the apple she had had the best meal in her life.

Onwards and upwards, soon the passage became narrower. The illuminated wall art flickered then disappeared and the stream became but a thin trickle.

Pan stopped, he seemed almost out of breath and Amelie realised that in his own way he had been carrying her all this time. The roof was very close now, she was suddenly claustrophobic and felt trapped. There was a rumble above, dust, debris, and some water came cascading down.

'Bother, bother, too careless, sloppy, very sloppy.'

Pan was cross with himself, snatched Amelie to his chest to protect her as more stones, quite big ones now, came crashing past them but not actually touching them. As things quieted down, he put her onto his shoulder and then lifted her through a small hole in the roof.

Amelie scrabbled onto firm ground there was dust all around her. She was suddenly afraid again.

It was very dark; she couldn't see anything and was

now finding her lungs filling with dust. The noises all around her were frightening, it sounded like wherever she was… was falling. There was a huge crash very nearby and a large beam or something seemed to have just missed her. She would have screamed but she couldn't get her breath. Suddenly she saw a shaft of light and started in that direction but tripped over a large object on the floor. She put her hand on the object to steady herself to get back up on her feet, and it was sort of not hard like she had expected.

As Hans Solo used to say in Star Wars, she suddenly had a bad feeling about this. She felt around the outline and knew at once it was a body…. there was another crash, and more light came in. She could see more now, it was a woman, lying on her back, a beautiful but old face. Thin long wispy yellow hair, and…. her heart missed a beat... not breathing. Her face white with plaster and dusty open staring eyes. If she could have done, she would have shrieked, but instead she jumped up and staggered unsteadily towards the light.

She could see figures, children, and an older man, she tried to walk towards them but felt her legs giving way but was aware that someone had caught her just before she lost consciousness.

It was the sound of a galloping horse that seemed

to wake her, a man she almost didn't know was shaking her and crying. He did not seem pleased to see her.

"Who are you? Who are you? Where is Madelaine?"

Chapter 27

Like being in a story

Amelie coughed a lot, and eventually got her breath. She had been dropped unceremoniously on the grass by the man who didn't seem to like her. Sitting up and looking around she saw a horseman disappearing into the woods and turned to find herself staring at a boy who was staring back at her.

It was Luka! His jaw dropped and eyes popped in surprise.

'Esme look here, it's Amelie, it really is.'

Esme was wrenched abruptly from her staring after the rapidly disappearing Edgar to being faced with a ghost like sister sitting on the grass. Roderick came between them and glowered at Amelie.

'You should be Madelaine, but you aren't, tis nature swapping things again, to be sure tis a trickster world we live in......you seen her? ...'

He saw from the expression she had, and that such an expression meant nothing good. His shoulders dropped, and his neck bent forward in anticipation of bad news, he stuttered, not wanting to hear the reply....

'She's dead, she is ain't she?'

Amelie, with tears beginning to fill her eyes, only nodded.

There was more crashing of falling masonry and they all retreated to watch the rest of the old farmhouse finally collapse.

When it was over there was an eerie silence, not even a bird cheeped. The three children who had had such different experiences to date just stared at the wreckage and wondered what was to become of them.

A movement in the long grass to the left of them caught their attention. They strained to make out who or what it was. Luka was first to spot a pair of odd long ears deep in the grass.

'It's Liplop, it is I bet you.'

And of course, it was, the real one. For once he ignored the children and went straight to the disconsolate Roderick. There was some conversation, but they could not hear it. Amelie was on her feet by now brushing off the plaster while still coughing up lots of unpleasant dust.

Esme direct as ever, asked if she had seen Madelaine's body. Amelie glumly admitted she had but did not want to elaborate.

She was still so confused, after all it was only

minutes ago that she had been pushed through the floor by the Great God Pan then immediately confronted with a beautiful but dead lady. She wanted to cry, to scream or just to see her old horse Rooster and ride away…. far away. But all she did was sit on the grass and stare at the crumbled old house.

Roderick Usher finished talking to the hare and turned to the children. He looked very sad and seemed to be struggling to find words to say. Perhaps not too surprising in one who has just lost a loved one and seen their house collapse. Amelie stared, without understanding the depth of his disaster.

This incarnation of Roderick was a not quite real person who had experienced a real disaster. He, being unused to such an unusual and unexpected reversal of events was totally distraught.

 She felt very sorry for him and tried to say something of comfort, but, like him, could not find any words. Esme was thinking about Edgar and Luka was trying to get Liplop's attention.

There was a humming. It was a while before everyone heard it. Luka turned to see Liplop stiffen and fix his gaze on the trees to the side of the old house. The humming got louder and formed into a faint song or chant.

Roderick turned, slumped onto the grassy slope thrusting his head into his hands.

'The Formorians, wouldn't you know it, the flipping Formorians.'

The chanting was getting louder and there was a silverish glow in the woods.

Luka was afraid, was it those same Formorians who had chased Grandpa and him on Colmer's Hill?

He edged near to Liplop for comfort but was shaken to find that the hare was trembling.

Esme was not afraid, just curious, after all she had met King Arthur, Merlin, Morgana Le Fey and had boulders thrown at her by giants, so what were a few more strange mythical creatures. She was beginning to feel all this was dream anyway it was too unreal. What was it Edgar had written?

'Is all that we see or seem, but a dream within a dream?'

Amelie too was not easily overawed anymore, but perhaps she should have been.

A tall thin transparent greenish woman was leading the column, she appeared to be wearing nothing at all. As she neared her scale was easier to judge, she really was tall, Luka reckoned about average house height. More worrying was in the distance behind her were two very big figures, still in the trees but taller than them by some margin, real giants, two to three houses high.

Liplop was staring at them and making frightened hairy noises. Luka could tell he wanted to run but was torn with staying to protect the children. Though it was obvious that nothing, but a very large tank could be much protection. The ground shook with every step.

There was a buzzing increasing in intensity as the fairies got closer, soon it was so loud as to stop anyone thinking.

Buzz, buzz……. Buzz. Liplop was chanting, softly at first, getting louder with the buzzing. It was a spell; they could tell that. Louder and louder as if the hare was challenging the fairies, suddenly pfzzzzt! …...Someone had switched off the lights.

Amelie woke up first, where was she?

It was still dark, very dark, black in fact, but she recognised the sound and the smell. Yet another cavern, damp, drippy, tinkling, was it the one she had been in before?

She felt her feet… not tied up then… and as she

was feeling around… she touched another figure. She felt up the body that was laid out flat on its back, as she got to the face the there was a snuffling and shaking of head to stop the annoyance. She recognised the spluttering with some relief…. it was sister Esme she knew with absolute certainty.

On the other side someone was coughing, it was a boy's cough, Luka! So, they were all ok, she thought. Then another thought arrived, perhaps this was not, OK?

A nasty thought wormed its way in, could it be a dungeon? Or like that horrid Oubliette in Corfe Castle…... were they going to rot here?

'Anybody here?'

Shouted a small boys voice, several degrees squeakier than he would have liked.

'Yes me, and Esme is here too, she is still asleep.'

'No, I am not, and thanks for poking up my nose.'

'Where are we?'

Luka cried with a tinge of desperation in his tone.

'It's a cave I think'.

'Could be a dungeon.'

Esme sniffed loudly.

'Hmmm, smells a bit, I don't know, well animally, could be a stables… has anyone got some sort of light?'

Did not smell like horses to Amelie.

'Do you think the Fairies have walled us in?'

Asked Luka, more a thought than a question.

'What if we are to be fresh food for the giants?'

Added Esme helpfully.

As if on cue there was aloud groaning noise, if they could have seen each other they would have seen them all jump nervously. They soon realised that the groaning noise was not a person but a very large door creaking on its hinges.

The door was so big, or they were so small, that they could hardly see the top of it. A bright bilious yellow light flooded in, momentarily blinding them.

There was a sound of laughter, the nervous sort, perhaps anticipating an event about to happen.

Chapter 28

The Amphitheatre

The door took an unconscionable long time to open, slowly revealing a huge amphitheatre...... so big that their eyes could not quite take it all in.

People, hundreds of them, were sitting in half circles, layer upon layer......and they were all looking at them!

A great roar went up, no not the crowd, a true roar. Like living lions make. All of them instantly knew this was not good....in fact it was obviously very bad indeed.

They had all seen the film Gladiator and knew this was an arena that was ok to sit in...... but not so good to be on the sand and the centre of attention.

There was a grunting and scraping behind them. Esme turned to see three large lightly armoured men waving tridents and nets. She screamed.... taking no notice, they began pushing the children into the arena with their fork tips. Driven into the blazing, blinding, sunshine, and oh.... it was so very hot.

The guards retreated, the door closed behind them with a deep reverberating thud, and they were alone. Well, that is except for 5 lions in a cage in the middle of semicircle, four lioness and a huge full maned male.

They stared at them; they all knew that deep down this was a fairy story, but would that stop them being eaten? Quite spontaneously they linked hands…. looked into each other's eyes… and said as one…. with as much chutzpa as they could manage …. 'We must be brave.'

Esme drew her rusty old sword, Luka felt in his pocket and pulled out his pathetically small little fairy knife.

Amelie stiffened her back and tried to remember Elizabeth's speech to the troops at Tilbury before the Spanish Armada in 1588.

'In the midst and heat of the battle, to live and die amongst you all; to lay down for my God, and for my kingdom, and my people, my honour, and my blood, even in the dust.

I know I have the body but of a weak and feeble woman; but I have the heart and stomach of a King, and of a King of England too!

I think foul scorn that Formaria or Mordred, or any prince of Fairy Land should dare to invade the borders of my realm to which rather than any dishonour shall grow by me. I myself will take up arms. I myself will be your general, judge, and rewarder of every one of your virtues in the field!'

As she finished one of the lion keepers brushed past her and left his Trident on the cage. Amelie almost without thinking grabbed it and waived it aloft like a true warrior queen.

Esme…. in her head she was Boadicea! Another indomitable British heroine, Queen of the Iceni, who had defeated a whole Roman army. In that terrifying moment she was determined to do her very best and not show fear to these evil fairies who had placed her here. She might have lacked a chariot, but her hair was streaming, there was a wild glint in her eye and wait…. yes…. the little rusty sword was shining in the sunlight.

Waiving it round her head she made silver gleaming patterns that hung in the scalding afternoon air and blinded those that stared. The magic was back!

Luka, surprisingly calm, rehearsed his speech in his head, or was it out loud?

'My name is Luka Bozic Vittorio, Commander of the Armies of the Pokémon, General of the Mandalorian Legions, loyal servant to the true Queen, Elizabeth Rex. Brother to a missing sister, friend to a famous ghost. And I will have my vengeance, in this life or the next!'

As he finished the little knife had become another glorious sword, terrifying and beautiful at the same time.

The roaring was by now deafening but now it was not the lions, it really was the crowd. They were all on their feet and throwing multitudes of cushions into the arena. They did not want to see such brave children horribly eaten by ravening beasts.

There was a collective gasp of horror as the lion keeper released the cage door and ran for safety behind a barrier in the wall, where his two companions were already safely ensconced. The children stood close together and the lions looked at them.

The male lion raised himself up, stared curiously at the small humans waiving shiny pointy things and seemed to turn to his wives. Perhaps wisely seeking their opinion.

'I hope he is not called Wallace, that's the lion that ate Albert in one those daft northern poems grandad likes.'*

Thought Esme.

Wallace or whoever seemed in no hurry. Normally the crowd would have been impatient but this time the mob was clearly on the side of the spirited children. A sort of nervous anticipatory hush fell over assembly. Then a tiny little

'Noooooooo!'

Echoed from the middle rows.

Yaya, sitting in the crowd, had recognised them! In seconds she was clambering over the people in front and was soon at the top of the wall that marked out the arena.

She was surprised to find Lea and Anna firmly at her side. Then she found herself confused and uncertain, what was she to do?

If she jumped into the ring wouldn't the lions just eat her too?

And what about her small companions? They would most likely jump with her and be eaten too. That would be her fault and, on her conscience forever. Though forever would not be very long in her case.

The crowd spotted what was happening and rather unkindly, given their initial reaction, began chanting,

'Jump, jump, jump.'

Luka took his eyes off the lions for a second and spotted Yaya just above him, easily close enough to recognise.

'Stay there! Don't jump.'

He yelled. The crowd disagreed.

'Jump, jump, jump.'

Anna decided it for them, with a half jump and half slide down the slightly angled wall she was at Luka's feet in no time, Lea followed, and so, with a final fatalistic shrug did Yaya. Soon all six children were huddled together staring at the still undecided lions.

The crowd was divided, some seem to have decided that if the children got eaten it would be quite exciting and they could go home for their tea.

They were now shouting for the lions to get on with it. The other half were on the children's side and were chanting for the lions to be locked up again.

Luka, searching round for an escape route, spotted an incongruous but familiar ice cream van, parked above the top row of seats. 2000 years before its time. A goatee bearded little man was selling ice creams to the people who would invent the stuff 1900 years later (the Italians). He waved a magnum at Luka and cackled. Time can be like that.

After his domestic conference Wallace seemed to reach a decision, turned, and started out of the cage in the direction of the children. But he was hardly out of the door when there was a tremor below his feet. This stopped him dead, there was fear in those deep black eyes, and it was not of the small children with pricky shiny things in front of him. The ground under the children wobbled like a jelly and they all fell over except little Anna who somehow kept her balance.

Now the crowd was screaming, there was panic, everyone trying to flee at once, but too afraid of being lion lunch to drop into the arena. The big lion roared, a terrible sound but there was fear in the cry. The lionesses rushed out of their cage heading straight for the children. Lea screamed, Amelie, on one knee, pointed her trident at them and Luka raised his by now impressive sword and stood in front of Lea. But the lions were too afraid to stop for a snack, they swerved, bolted over a collapsed piece of wall, and disappeared in the direction of the small town below.

There was a crumbling sound behind them, two huge columns crashed onto the sand and a one rolled perilously close to where they stood. The ground was still shaking but not as violently.

Freed from the fear of the lions, the children could look behind them and there was a sight!

It was Etna! The huge snow-capped volcano was in full eruption mode, there was an intense column of fire topped by a rapidly spreading, huge, heavy, and inky black cloud of volcanic ash.

As they stared, truly awestruck, at what seemed like the beginning of the end of the world, the sun went out. Just like switching a light off it went totally dark, and the air was filled with hot cloying dust.

Luka had at last recognised that this was Taormina in Sicily, which he knew well. His other grandad had lived there all his life and his mum had spent most of her childhood there. He felt comforted and knew that somehow, they would all be alright.

'Join hands' cried Amelie, taking charge as the oldest.

'We can't stay here…. We will all choke or be incinerated'.

Added Luka a trifle unnecessarily.

'I know where to go where we will be safer, I will lead you,' said Lea.

She seemed to have the ability to see in the dark as they stumbled over rocks and fallen masonry. Leading them down a path that avoided the main street, which was already blocked by collapsed houses and terrified screaming people.

The air was getting harder to breathe, and quite big lumps of hot glowing embers were falling all around. One nearly set Esme's hair alight, but Luka put it out quickly with just his hands.

'Here, here this way.'

In front of them was a beautiful building with a garden and a large pond full of exquisite cream water lilies, shining almost supernaturally in the stygian gloom. Esme dunked her head in the water to put out the last of the singeing and Luka cooled his painful hands.

'The lilies are called white lotus' said Lea matter of factly, something in Yaya's memory jogged, but she ignored it.

'Come on…. we must get down to the seashore... it will be safer there, down here……'

She pointed to a little path at the end of the garden. Very quickly it became very steep, they slipped a lot, and though it was still very dark the children were aware that if one fell, probably they all fell. The drop was fearsome. It really was an awfully long way down, but little Anna, who had the balance of a mountain goat, led the way.

After what seemed like an age they scrambled onto the beach; the sea was rough from the earthquake and the breakers were crashing nearby. There was a narrow little causeway, illuminated now by this unearthly glow emanating from an angry Etna. Anna fearlessly ran over it first, showing them the way. Sea spray was all around, and underfoot was very treacherous.

'Take it in turns' Lea said,

'There is a cave on the other side, we can hide in there till the worst is over. I go crabbing there quite a lot.'

Yaya followed Anna and sort of recognised the place, though it had changed in 2000 years, but not as much as she expected.

They all scrabbled over and found the shelter of a small temple carved into a cave a few feet above the sea, till only Luka and Esme were left.

His knife had shrunk and was back in his pocket, but Esme was still clutching her sword and using it as a steadying walking stick. Just as she was starting to cross a huge wave caught her and she was swept into the sea and out of sight. Luka stared and stared but she was nowhere to be seen.

Here is the full original.

The Lion and Albert

by Marriott Edgar (1880-1951)

There's a famous seaside place called Blackpool,

That's noted for fresh-air and fun,

And Mr and Mrs Ramsbottom

Went there with young Albert, their son.

A grand little lad was their Albert,

All dressed in his best; quite a swell,

With a stick with an 'orse's 'ead 'andle,

The finest that Woolworth's could sell.

They didn't think much to the ocean:

The waves, they was fiddlin' and small

There was no wrecks and nobody drownded,

'Fact, nothing to laugh at at all.

So, seeking for further amusement,

They paid and went into the zoo

Where they'd lions and tigers and camels

And old ale and sandwiches too.

There were one great big lion called Wallace;

His nose was all covered with scars.

He lay in a som-no-lent posture

With the side of his face on the bars.

Now Albert had heard about lions,

How they was ferocious and wild.

To see Wallace lying so peaceful,

Well... it didn't seem right to the child.

So straight 'way the brave little feller,

Not showing a morsel of fear,

Took 'is stick with the 'orse's 'ead 'andle

And shoved it in Wallace's ear!

You could see that the lion didn't like it,

For giving a kind of a roll,

He pulled Albert inside the cage with 'im

And swallowed the little lad... whole!

Then Pa, who had seen the occurrence,

And didn't know what to do next,

Said, "Mother! Yon lions 'et Albert."

And Mother said "Eeh, I am vexed!"

Then Mr and Mrs Ramsbottom —

Quite rightly, when all's said and done —

Complained to the Animal Keeper

That the lion had eaten their son.

The keeper was quite nice about it;

He said, "What a nasty mishap.

Are you sure that it's your boy he's eaten?"

Pa said, "Am I sure? There's his cap!"

So the manager had to be sent for.

He came and he said, "What's to do?"

Pa said, "Yon lion's 'et Albert,

And 'im in his Sunday clothes, too."

Then Mother said, "Right's right, young feller;

I think it's a shame and a sin

For a lion to go and eat Albert

And after we've paid to come in!"

The manager wanted no trouble.

He took out his purse right away,

Saying, "How much to settle the matter?"

Pa said "What do you usually pay?"

But Mother had turned a bit awkward

When she thought where her Albert had gone.

She said, "No! Someone's got to be summonsed!"

So that was decided upon.

Then off they went to the P'lice Station

In front of a Magistrate chap.

They told 'im what happened to Albert,

And proved it by showing his cap.

The Magistrate gave his o-pinion

That no-one was really to blame.

He said that he hoped the Ramsbottoms

Would have further sons to their name.

At that Mother got proper blazing,

And "Thank you, sir, kindly!" said she.

"What?! Waste all our lives raising children

To feed ruddy lions? Not me!"

Chapter 29

A Quinquereme

It was still dark, the sea was very rough, large glowing boulders of lava were starting to fall from the sky and Esme was gone!

Luka kept staring into the waves, and suddenly he saw a thin beam of light like a Jedi light saber. Esme's sword! He was a good swimmer and went swimming every day if he could. Without hesitation he dived into the churning sea and headed for the light. It was hard to swim, the currents were strong, and the surface of the water was gritty with powdered pumice, drops of solidified lava.

Luka didn't care, what was important was to save Esme. After a few strokes he got into his stride and cut through the water like a demented shark.

The light saber was just slipping from view, below the surface, when he reached her. She was limp, the sword had slipped from her hand, and Luka had to paddle furiously to lift her head clear of the water. Relief surged through him as he felt her gasp in a lungful of smoky air.

He managed to paddle walk her to the shallows and pulled her up onto the beach near the cave. A huge lump of hot lava crashed into the sea where they had just been.

This seemed to wake Esme up and she sat up coughing and spluttering. Luka yanked her to her feet and within moments they were safe inside with all the others.

'A Muntagna is very angry.' Said a quiet little Anna.

'We normally call her Mongibello but not now, she is not beautiful today.'

No one at that moment could think of anything else useful to say, so they sat watching the ashfall huddled together, at least it wasn't cold.

Esme was grieving over the loss of her magic sword but very grateful for her cousin's dramatic intervention. Slowly they all realised that they were very hungry and thirsty too. Time suddenly began to matter.

A loud scraping sound nearby grabbed their attention. Yaya went to look and was amazed to find a huge wooden ship, she thought it 50 metres or so long, with three banks of oars that were being rapidly withdrawn inside. A few of them were obviously snapped so this was obviously not an intended stop. Amelie came to see, and her jaw dropped.

'Gosh, it's a Quinquereme.... a real one! .... it is so

big! ...... wow it's amazing!'

 Esme poked her head out and stared in joy.... of all the sites she had yet seen, seeing a real genuine old Roman cargo ship seemed just about the best.

The words came to her.

'Quinquereme of Nineveh from distant Ophir,

Rowing home to haven in sunny Palestine,

With a cargo of ivory,

And apes and peacocks,

Sandalwood, cedarwood, and sweet white wine.'*

A burst of angry shouting shook her from her reverie. It was quickly apparent that the crew were not so happy as she. The argument was on board and a couple of sailors in loose clothing scrambled out of an opened port on to the beach, waving angrily and pointing.

Etna was quieting, the wind had changed, whisps of

265

light pierced the gloom, and soon the sun made an appearance. The children crowded at the entrance staring at the huge gleaming wooden ship. The sand was black, covered in volcanic ash, and they could now see that the stern of the ship was ablaze.

'They have been hit by a lava bomb.'

Said Luka with the absolute certainty of smart-arse young boys, but in truth it turned out he was right. (for once)

They watched as there was much rushing about. The men soon formed a relay of scooping buckets of seawater and passing them along the line to be quickly poured on the flames. They had the fire under control very quickly, it was quite impressive.

A few more sailors were on the shore and now a full dressed Roman Captain joined them. He began to inspect the damage to gauge how well or badly the ship was beached.

With plumed helmet, bronze chest armour, the roman kilt, and a short stabbing sword in his belt, he looked very grand and exuded an air of superior pomposity. His mannerisms would have reminded Grandad of Captain Mainwaring in Dad's Army.

He suddenly spotted the children and gestured to some sailors to go and fetch them to him. Soon all the six were staring at the Roman Master as he wrinkled his nose and stared back at them.

'And what pray are you lot doing here?'

Luka heard him in Croatian, Lea in Italian and Amelie and Esme in Strine. They all understood but had no immediate answer to what was, Yaya reckoned anyway, a pretty stupid question. She answered her own question, perhaps one day she will be a politician.

'Er Mr Captain, can we have something to drink we are very thirsty. Some crisps would be good too.'

The Master was non plussed but barked an order to a lesser minion who rushed off inside the ship.

'Where is this place?' He asked a trifle less certainly.

'Taormina'

Said Lea, he heard 'Taorminium.' He looked a bit shaken; this was obviously not where he was expecting to be.

'Messina!! Not Messina.'

He was shaking his head and was obviously very cross but who with?

Luka knew that someone was going to get it in the

neck, almost certainly the navigator who was probably keeping out of everyone's way, especially the captain.

A big burly sailor appeared with a flask under one arm and a dish covered in roman goodies. He looked at the captain and placed it in front of the famished group. They fell upon it; the food was surprisingly snacky and delicious. Another sailor brought some wooden cups and started filling them with a sweet sticky wine while, yet another sailor topped up with an amphora of brackish water. The result was delicious and very thirst quenching.

'It must be alcoholic.' said Luka.

'Yes, but not much, I think. They need the alcohol to keep it sort of sterile, which was hard in the old days.' Added Amelie.

'These are the old days aren't they. How do we get back to our days, that's the question?'

Said Yaya looking a bit worried.

Luka took another cupful and began feeling distinctly mellow. There was definitely alcohol in the drink. Esme joined him and soon they were quite giggly. Amelie came over all bossy and suggested enough was enough. She was right of course, but sometimes being right isn't everything.

They watched as the Captain bossed his sailors around, and a group with huge oars started trying to lever the ship off the beach.

'Have you noticed how small they all are?' Said Esme

'They are, aren't they.' Agreed Luka, and of course it was true. None of the Romans were much above 5foot 6. Amelie was already taller than all of them.

'Nelson was only 5ft 4. But on his column in Trafalgar Square in London he is a giant at 18ft (5.5m)'

Esme contributed without any clear reason why.

Small they may have been, but straightforward they weren't. Yaya noticed that the crew were talking and that they kept looking at the children. Their looks were not reassuring, a bit like a tiger sizing up her prey.

'Lea, Anna get out of here now, something is up, and you must stay safe, go on quickly run back home.'

Fortunately, they took her advice and took off without demur. In no time they were disappearing out of site up the cliff path.

Amelie had seen Yaya send the little ones off and

began to sense the fear. She too started noticing how the romans were looking at them. Were they going to take them prisoner?

An even nastier thought crept into her mind. Were they going to enslave them? She remembered that the romans had slaves and realised that they were ideal material, young healthy and unable to resist. She suspected they would fetch a good price.

This was exactly the same conclusion the sailors had come to. A group was speaking to the Master who was looking in their direction. Amelie caught Yaya's eye and they both nodded at each other…. they had to get away… and quickly!

Sadly, Luka and Esme were not so on the ball, probably due to drinking too much roman cordial.

Amelie and Yaya turned to them. In a whisper that was far too loud Amelie said.

'They are all eyeing us up, I think they mean to take us prisoner, perhaps make us slaves, we have to get out of here.'

'Come on,'

Encouraged Yaya leading from the front.

Esme and Luka were a bit slower, and Esme was still looking around for her precious sword. Then she saw it, sticking out of a clump of seaweed only a few yards away. Before anyone could stop her, she was off, but she was not quick enough.

The big sailor spotted the commotion and grabbed her before she reached the spot. A group of sailors quickly surrounded the remaining three. Struggling proved useless, the romans were strong, and their wrists were lashed in seconds. They were led towards the galley. Luka wondered if he would be chained to an oar and die of exhaustion, after all he had watched Ben Hur twice. The girls were terrified as to what being a slave would mean. Despair shrouded them, they felt so alone and abandoned.

*Cargoes (1903)

John Masefield

Quinquireme of Nineveh from distant Ophir,

Rowing home to haven in sunny Palestine,

With a cargo of ivory,

And apes and peacocks,

Sandalwood, cedarwood, and sweet white wine.

Stately Spanish galleon coming from the Isthmus,

Dipping through the Tropics by the palm-green shores,

With a cargo of diamonds,

Emeralds, amythysts,

Topazes, and cinnamon, and gold moidores.

Dirty British coaster with a salt-caked smoke stack,

Butting through the Channel in the mad March days,

With a cargo of Tyne coal,

Road-rails, pig-lead,

Firewood, iron-ware, and cheap tin trays.

Chapter 30

A narrow escape and a very strange journey

The big sailor went to retrieve the sword from the seaweed, only to find it firmly stuck. He tugged at it a couple of times but after failing to budge it, called to the group escorting the children, who stopped and turned. A couple went over to the sword and again failed to move it. Esme smiled to herself, with an idea forming in her mind.

'Get ready to run everyone, I have an idea.'

Luka was doubtful and did not fancy one of those long very sharp spears in his back, like that chap Sir Mortimer had dug up.

'Run where?'

Yaya was definite.

'Back to the cave, I am sure it goes much deeper, something in my bones tells me we will get away from them in there.'

Esme shouted at the sailors.

'It is my sword so I should get it.'

All of them had another go, not wishing to give a chance to a silly girl who did not have a prayer of loosening it. Eventually the Master saw what was happening and strutted across and grabbed the hilt with the absolute expectation of freeing it with one pull. Because of his total certainty and failure to countenance failure when he pulled unsuccessfully…. he fell over. A few of the crew sniggered, and the children laughed out loud. He was furious, tried twice more with increasing effort and frustration. On the final time, he ended up sitting on his bottom on the black sand.

The sword seemed to be glinting a bit more in the sunshine while remaining firmly unmoved.

The sailors were openly laughing now, and Esme took the opportunity to slip away. She soon reached the rock. Quickly and cleverly, she cut the leather wrist straps using the upright blade. Grabbing the sword handle she easily lifted it from the seaweed covered stone, no effort required. She waved it round her head in a gesture of triumph which was of course, at the same time, a signal to run for it.

'This my magic sword and if you come near me, it will do you harm.'

She poked at the still seated Master who flinched dramatically. The kids were off running and reached the cave mouth in no time. Esme backed off jabbing her weapon at the men and when they showed no sign of rushing her, turned and ran too.

As they stood united in the cave entrance the Roman's bravery returned and with a group yell, they chased along the beach to recapture their valuable treasure. The romans were quicker than they expected. One managed to grab Esme and she dropped her sword, Luka trying to help too, was caught. Yaya and Amelie unsure what to do, hesitated too long and were grabbed...... but then fate intervened.

There was a loud roaring. The roman captain disappeared under a huge male lion; his prolonged scream was cut short by a loud crunching sound. The crew panicked, surrounded by four hungry lioness they dropped their captives and began to run back to their ship. The lions ignored the children, not wanting a snack but a full lunch.

Esme grabbed her sword, and they hurried to the cave entrance. Amelie tried not to look but couldn't keep the screams out. Even though they had wanted to enslave her she felt sorry for the sailors. Luka stared at the carnage, horrified but fascinated, Yaya pulled him into the cave.

'Come on, they will come for us next.'

She said turning and leading the way deeper inside. Everyone followed, beings a lion's lunch did not appeal. Soon the cave entrance was just a little circle of light behind them. Esme's sword was again giving a faint light, but Yaya was still leading the way. Just as she was slowing up due to the gathering gloom, she felt a soft paw take her hand. It was hard to see who it was, a black panther in a cave is a good disguise.

'Follow me, quickly, follow me.'

In no time at all they were in total darkness, the shouts of their pursuers became fainter and fainter.

Bast, the Egyptian Cat Goddess, for that is who it was, continued to lead Yaya. Esme's sword shone a dim silver light so that they could see, just, that the cave walls were covered in picture writing, like Egyptian hieroglyphics but not quite the same.

Yaya felt Bast push something into her hand then she was gone, she slowed, hesitated and suddenly her feet were wet. In front of her was water, it was shimmering in a ghostly very pale blue, and was very still. In her hand was a tiny little purse.

'Stop everyone, we have reached a lake I think, but I am not sure what we are supposed to do.'

Everyone peered into the eerie fluttering light, but all was still. They sat down to wait for something to happen.

There was shouting in the tunnel behind them,

some of the sailors had taken the same escape route as the children. It sounded like there was quite a lot of them.

Yaya looked in the purse, there were four gold coins, freshly minted and gleaming. Esme had taken up position at the rear because she had the sword. Luka scrabbled around for his little fairy knife but on this occasion, very disappointingly, that is exactly what it remained. Amelie's heart sank, so they were going to be slaves after all, it seemed too unfair, and if anything, she felt worse this time. It is always the hope that is the killer.

The shouting was getting very close. The flickering flames making weird frightening shadows, then there was a light, gentle lapping noise behind them. A tall thin extremely creepy figure in a hooded gown was rapidly approaching on a narrow flat boat. He used a long pole to propel it at quite some speed and was beached in no time. Yaya went to scramble aboard but the figure extended a bony arm to stop her.

'Payment.'

The figure croaked in an unearthly voice. Yaya panicked; the sailors were now only 50 metres away.

'What's the fare?'

And instantly she knew exactly what the fare was. She handed the gold coins to the ferryman. He took the purse, seemed to take an age to study it, then beckoned them on to the punt.

They were only just all aboard when the leading roman threw a spear, it was heading straight for Yaya. She prepared for the pain and closed her eyes, but nothing happened.

If she had kept her eyes open, she would have seen the figure pluck the spear from the air and throw it straight back in one easy motion. The thrower was himself impaled and stared open mouthed as he pitched, quite dead, into the lake. This awed the chasing company, and becoming much more cautious began pointing at the boatman.

'It's Charon I tell you, those on that boat are all dead.' Said one

'If they've paid, they might be ok, otherwise he will have their souls.'

Another jumped in the water to try a grab the boat and immediately was turned to stone and sank like one too.

Luka was trying to look at the figure with the pole, but he didn't seem to have a face. Under the cowl was just darkness, he shivered. This was seriously spooky.

The boat moved silently and surprisingly fast. Charon was not a chatty individual. In truth he made no sound at all, though his rhythmic pushing of the pole seemed to involve no effort.

They were not out in the open, in fact it was very claustrophobic, as the roof was always just a metre or two above the boat. It was not pitch black either, a ghostly blue light was everywhere.

Amelie remembered the old film about the white whale, Moby Dick, and the sequence when the ship was covered in blue flame. St Elmo's fire, and this was the same light. Charon seemed to shimmer with it. Luka touched the water, and his hand became alight with blue cold flame. Looking behind he saw they were leaving a wondrous trail of flickering iridescence.

No one spoke, it didn't seem the time, minutes, then hours passed, perhaps even days. It was not a short journey.

Amelie had thought this must be the fabled river Styx, but it was too wide for a river, it was certainly a lake, even possibly a sea.

No one was hungry, no one was thirsty, and no one needed the loo. It was as if time was passing but it wasn't. Thinking sort of stopped too, their minds emptied, Esme had just one line on a repeating loop going round in her head.

'As idle as a painted ship upon a painted ocean.'*

The ancient mariner would have understood.

Eventually the blue began to fade, other colours fought for space, particularly orange, gray and perhaps green. There was a smell, a smoky perfumed smell. They all recognised it and suddenly thoughts came back. It was pipe smoke, and they knew who's pipe it was.

Looking forward they could all see a familiar figure standing at what appeared to the entrance to wherever they were. There he was with his huge orange pipe, a genuine Meerschaum he had proudly told them, and his very carefully coiffured handlebar moustache. They all saw him; he was not letting his inner elf out this time.

The boat scraped up onto the shore. The kids rushed off and when Yaya looked back there was no ferryman, in fact there was no boat, and she was staring at a solid cliff.

It was much colder than Taormina. They were again standing on a beach, and it was nearly dark. It took a while to work out if it was sunset or daybreak. It was the latter.

Sir Mortimer was standing in front of a strange, almost circular, arched rock in the sea behind him, just a 100 metres away. As they looked at him, they saw a most wonderful sight. The sun was just appearing on the edge of the waves, when there was a moment that the whole sea flashed an emerald green. Then the orb rose and flooded the arch with blazing red rays and a piercing, blinding, bolt of sunlight illuminated the four children. As if a message from God. Perhaps it was.

Yaya was awestruck and in the next moment realised she was cold. She looked at her arms and saw them covered in goosebumps. Amelie was first to put voice to the feeling.

'Jees it's so cold. We must be back in England'.

They could see lots of small boats out on the sea, the were some flashes too. Perhaps it was a regatta? thought Amelie.

'Ah, so sorry, colder than I expected for the time of

year, I have some rugs in the car.'

Exclaimed sir Mortimer in his best plummy Oxford voice.

'Best get out of here. The walk up the hill will warm you up. Did you enjoy the sunrise here at Durdle Door? A very fine one today, with a green flash no less. Let's hope it is a good omen.'

*A tiny bit of

The Ancient Mariner

By Samuel Taylor Coleridge 1836

The fair breeze blew, the white foam flew,

The furrow followed free;

We were the first that ever burst

Into that silent sea.

Down dropt the breeze, the sails dropt down,

'Twas sad as sad could be;

And we did speak only to break

The silence of the sea!

All in a hot and copper sky,

The bloody Sun, at noon,

Right up above the mast did stand,

No bigger than the Moon.

Day after day, day after day,

We stuck, nor breath nor motion;

As idle as a painted ship

Upon a painted ocean.

Water, water, every where,

And all the boards did shrink;

Water, water, every where,

Nor any drop to drink.

Chapter 31

Bombed!

The children were all hoping this adventure was coming to an end. It had been very exciting and what stories they would have to tell.... but going home...... and a nice peaceful boring holiday now seemed very attractive. You can have too much excitement.

Eventually they wheezed and puffed up the extremely steep cliff path only to find at the top a couple of very old-fashioned looking cars and a battered old caravan that looked like it had been new before the flood.

Amelie turned back to look at the sea.... there were still lots of little boats.... now clearly funneling into a harbour, Weymouth she thought. They were not yachts, more like cabin cruisers, and they were crammed full of people, even on the roofs, many more than seemed safe. As she stared, she became aware of an irregular distant banging sound. Deep down she immediately knew it for what it was.... gunfire. Her heart sank. This was war...... she wasn't sure which one, but little boats full of soldiers rang a distant bell.

Yaya was studying Sir Mortimer. He was definitely younger, fitter and less, well, old mannish. Much more Sherlock Holmes really.

Out of breath as she was, she whispered to Luka in between gasps.

'I don't think we are out of this story yet. See...... he looks much younger, and the cars, they are ancient. I don't think we are back in our time yet.'

He opened the front and rear door of a small, dark red, car and gestured them to climb in.

'Come on chaps, my trusty Austin 7 we need to get

out of the open it is not safe around here.'

It was tiny, almost a toy, how on earth could they all fit into that flimsy little tin can? But they managed, surprisingly easily.

Luka was looking around for malevolent fairies, and Esme for Mordred's men, but the present made itself felt in the shape of a large twin engine propeller aircraft that swooped just over the top of them. The plane, being so close, was extremely loud and very scary! Everyone ducked reflexly....as if that would help.

Esme even recognised it from multiple trips to aircraft museums.

'Gosh that's a Junker Ju 88.'

'A what?' exclaimed Amelie.

'A German light bomber from the Second world war. You could see the white trimmed black cross on the fuselage.'

'Your sister is quite correct, and I fear he is not done with us.'

Said Sir M trying to start the car but having some difficulty. He kept turning the key on the dashboard, the car coughed, jerked but the engine refused to start. Luka, peering out of the passenger side rear window, spotted that the aircraft had turned and was coming back, as if for them!

He spluttered an undignified sort of 'ARRRGHH.'

But at last, the little car appreciated the urgency of the situation, the engine spluttered into life and off they shot. Sir Mortimer's foot was pressing the accelerator pedal to the floor.

'Get down everyone, this could get a little rough.'

The car was going quite quickly now, passing through a small village. There was a screaming sound of a bomb falling, but it landed behind them. Then there was a huge explosion and part of the soft roof of the car peeled off, but they stayed on the road.

'Oh, my car, my lovely car, damn those Jerries. Still, they haven't done for us. I don't think he will try again, or our Spitfires will get him.'

When it seemed safe the children climbed back onto the seats. They all looked for seatbelts but there weren't any.

'When are we?'

Asked Yaya, and everyone laughed as it seemed such a queer question, but everyone knew what she meant.

'Tuesday June the fourth 1940.'

'Oh gosh, that's Dunkirk time.'

Said Esme in a quiet low voice. Luka remembered

the film vaguely. Lots of soldiers standing round on beaches being bombed, climbing into hundreds of small boats, and being shot at by Germans.

Amelie, suddenly angry and fed up exclaimed:

'I thought this adventure was about some way to get back to peacefulness, stopping a war, restoring balance and harmony. If that is so we seem to be in the wrong time entirely, perhaps even the wrong place.'

Esme suddenly shouted,

'Maine, this is Maine, I recognise it. Edgar and I came through here.'

She tailed off but Luka completed her sentence.

'120 years ago, it is called Broadmayne now.'

Amelie and Yaya realised they had a lot to catch up on.

'Edgar who?'

Asked Amelie, but it wasn't the time. Esme and Luka lapsed into silence, up one valley down another and soon they were driving up Dorchester High West Street.

Luka tried to see if the Teddy Bear museum was open, but though he recognised the house it was obviously not a museum and there were no lurking bears that he could see. The street was recognisable, but all the windows were blacked out and it was very joyless. After a mile or so there was the Hill fort on the right. There seemed to be some sort of army camp there now, they drove into it.

Sir Mortimer stopped the car and lifted a long, strange lever that squeaked as he pulled it.

'Ruddy handbrake is a bit stiff, need to take the old girl to the garage, get her sorted and the roof fixed.'

Seemingly far more worried about his car than anything else. He sat at the wheel and stared straight ahead for a while. It was mainly fields. Luka could see a farmhouse far to his left, and although he did not recognise it, he knew the site.

That was where the wall had collapsed, and they had fled the Formorians with the giants. Esme recognised it too.

'They have rebuilt the farm.'

She said to herself, but Amelie heard.

'Oh! Is that where it was, I didn't really have much time to get my bearings. And then suddenly we were to be eaten by lions, it is all very confusing. I mean are we all mad?'

She suddenly turned on the driver.

'And as for you, just who the heck are you? I know you are not the real Sir Mortimer, but you are a doppelganger.'

'A what?' Interjected Yaya.

'A double, we know they are all shapeshifters, he is a fairy of some sort. I am not sure if he is good or bad, but I do know he is not who he pretends to be.'

'I think we are parked pretty close to where our grandparents live now.' Said Luka.

The ground rumbled underneath them, like in the Amphitheater. The car wobbled. Sir Mortimer slumped over the steering wheel and sighed.

'It's blocked here, this is the spot, but this is not the time. Needs digging, that's what I am supposed to be good at, digging, still digging……. He realised something was happening…... 'Quickly, quickly, get out but stay together, you must stay together.'

He was fading, becoming transparent. The children experienced a group fear, Sir Mortimer might be a bit strange, but he was a friend, and they did know him. Being on their own again would be very frightening. They piled out but the ground under them did not seem too firm. Doing nothing was obviously not an option.

'Come on'

Said Amelie grabbing the nearest hand which happened to be Yaya's.

'We have got to get off this bit of land, it is going to collapse I just know it.'

Everyone was on edge and finally tuned so needed no second call. They ran for it, and not a moment too soon!

A circle of earth, including the Austin Seven, folded in on itself. Luka slipped and nearly fell in, but Esme grabbed his arm as she anchored her sword, (yes, she still had it) in the firmer earth. With her help he managed to scrabble free. The little car disappeared into the depths, spinning as it fell and Esme caught the faintest glimpse of the tomb and the staircase they had run down, what seemed so long ago. As she stared the vision disappeared and the earth filled itself up again but not entirely.

'Oi, you lot, what do you think you are doin'?'

A large soldier with three stripes on his shirt sleeve appeared out of nowhere in front of them. He peered over the top of them at the still considerable hole that had so suddenly appeared.

'Gor blimey, that's a hole an no mistake! Youse lot are lucky, don't want to fall in one of them, never come out, ruddy sinkholes. This place is like a bloomin' rabbit warren, ruddy tunnels everywhere. Go on now get on home, your parents will be worried, this is no place for kids especially not today. We've got that sorry lot from Dunkirk who need some grub an' somewhere to kip. Half of them today are Frogs, no speaka the lingo…. say any of youse speak Frenchie?'

There was a communal shaking of heads, as far as Luka was concerned, he wasn't sure about his English either as he could not easily understand the sergeant.

The children just stood there, not sure where to go. The sergeant picked up on the confusion.

'Got no 'omes to go to. You didn't just appear out of nowhere so go back to where it was you comes from. This is army territory, and you should scram…. Go one then, gerroff.'

Still, no one moved. Amelie took it on herself to be spokesperson.

'Err… I am afraid that the fact is….err…. we don't have any homes to go to. We have been left here by someone who has deserted us and…. Well…we are in a bit of a pickle.'

'You can say that again! What am I meant to do with

abandoned kids?'

An idea seem to strike him.

'I know, I know, we will just have to process you as if you were on one of them boats, that's it…waifs and strays…flotsam and ruddy jetsam…. The army will have a form for it…. Right then with me. Now look 'ere, when they asks you, you were on the boats, got that…. You were on them boats.'

He led them through a forest of canvas bell tents and down to near the railway line. There was a tent in front of a big red brick wall, that did not seem to serve any obvious purpose.

'Shootin' range normally.'

In answer to Luka's querulous expression, who then immediately spotted lots of shiny brass rifle bullet cases round his feet, totally irresistible, he stopped to pick up a few.

'Not now, not now, this way, 'ere…in 'ere.'

A bookish scrawny soldier peered at them from behind a desk.

'Waifs and strays from Belgium I thinks, not much good at English.'

The sergeant turned in a very military way and winked at Yaya. She wondered if he was a real sergeant, there was just the faintest whiff of Sir Mortimer about him, almost as if he was trying too hard to seem like a cockney soldier.

Suddenly they heard a by now already too familiar sound. That of a Junker JU88, there was a groaning wailing noise.

'Air raid warning. On the floor!'

Bombs began falling and one was very close.

Boom!

Chapter 32

To the Woods.

Esme felt large lumps of soil landing on her. This was good she thought, at least I am still here. Shakily Luka got to his feet feeling as though he had been in a boxing ring and lost very badly. The ringing in his ears meant he could not hear anything. He could see Yaya trying to say something to him but being no good at lipreading, he just half smiled, managing only to look a bit gormless. Amelie was slumped forward, her long hair muddied and in disarray. Yaya was more numb than hurt, after getting no response from Luka she felt like crying but just couldn't summon up the energy.

Luka pulled her up and they hugged, just grateful to be alive. Esme pulled Amelie to her feet, and they looked around. Most of the tents were still there and it was clear that the stick of bombs had mostly fallen harmlessly near the river. The bomb that had nearly got them had landed behind the high wall of the rifle range and that had saved them. The tent they had been in was gone.

Yaya sort of woke up.

'I think we have to get away from here, they will come back, I am sure.'

No one made much response.

'Come on, in think I know where we will be safe.'

The sound of another air raiding warning suddenly shook the others into action.

'Come on...'

Yaya pulled Luka to get him started.

'Let's follow the railway line to the tunnel, we should be safe there.'

She scrambled through a mangled fence and onto the line, the others followed. The tunnel entrance was soon in view just a 100 metres or so, but they could hear the planes. Although they were running as fast as they could the distance did not seem to be getting much less and the planes were now almost overhead.

The first bombs were already on the way down, but at last the entrance was close. A man with a funny hat was waving at them from inside the tunnel, encouraging them to run ever faster.

There was a bang from up the hill...... then another...... two planes passed overhead...... that ghastly whining sound of a falling bomb ......another huge explosion......the ground shook...... they had made it...... but only just.

The man kept backing away and gestured for them to keep running. There was a side tunnel, he took them down there and as he did there was a huge explosion near the entrance.

He pulled them all in a little storage cupboard and slammed the door. Not a moment too soon. The door rattled and protested but the shock wave went harmlessly by, they were safe. Well sort of….

The storeroom smelt oily and was lit by a narrow little lamp surrounded by a wire gauze chimney. Amelie recognised it from a trip to a mining museum in Australia.

'That's a Davy Lamp.'

Which seemed an odd thing to say when they had all just been nearly blown to smithereens, but sometimes in real disasters it is the little things that seem important.

Yaya was studying the man in the funny stove pipe hat and of course she knew him. She had seen him before on the hill that day with Nona Judy that seemed so long ago now.

'Hello, I am Yaya, and you are Mr Isambard Kingdom Brunel if I am not mistaken.'

'Brunel will do miss.'

'But you are not really are you.'

Esme managed having just got her breath back,

'You're a fairy or an elf or something but you are not who you are pretending to be that is for sure.'

Mr Brunel seemed quite offended.

'I most certainly am. How can you doubt your own eyes?'

'Well after all the adventures we have been through we have learned not to trust what we see. As soon as we do, something else happens that proves it wrong or just confuses us...'

'You are not making any sense.'

'Well not to you maybe but what Esme is trying to say makes sense to us.'

Said Yaya.

'I mean just recently you pretended to be Sir Mortimer Wheeler, before that you were Merlin, or an angel, a strange god or something else, none of you is real...... it is all so weird.'

Mr Brunel was having none of it.

'Well, all I can tell you is that I am not used to being so disrespected. I have built ships, bridges, tunnels, and roads and intend to build more.

I have a calling and a talent and am currently only trying to help you escape from......'

He tailed off looking more uncertain and a little confused.

'What are you escaping from?.......Am I who I say I am?'......

He began to shimmer and become less solid.

'I am mister Brunel, tunnel builder extraordinary.... I really am....'

And he faded away as they stared.

Amelie looked thoughtful,

'I think he really did think he was who he said he was, until he thought about it. Then, when he came face to face with the obvious truth that he wasn't Isambard Brunel really...... the spirit in him could not maintain the illusion...... so he faded away. I mean he obviously meant well because he saved us from the bomb blast.'

'But was that real too? I mean maybe all that was just imagination or something.' Luka wondered.

'So where are we? And what time is it? You know big time and not small time, like which century? I think my brain hurts.' Yaya admitted.

Esme waived her sword, it shone and flashed in the dim light.

'Well, I still have my sword.'

She said proudly.

There was a rustling sound, as leaves in a forest. Yaya pointed and there was obviously an exit. They felt wind on their faces, but it was still very dark. A scurrying scrabbling noise, very close by, made Amelie scream.

'Oi, you.... watch me nuts! ... this is not a playground you know I flippin' live 'ere.'

Esme waived her sword to give them some light to see what sort of creature this was. A big red bushy tail gave it away.

'It's only a squirrel.'

'What do you mean only...' said the creature in a cross squirrely sort of voice and disappeared.

They were in the open now, but it was dark, there were twinkling stars in the night sky, and there were trees all around, but the moon was bright.

'Look.'

Esme waved her sword, pointing at a large cottage with a man standing in the doorway. He smiled, waved and as they approached said.

'Hmmm, I see you have made the natives restless. I hope he returns'.

This was a deeper cultured very English voice. They saw he was another character with a fine moustache.

'Who are you this time?' said Yaya in a challenging sort of way.

'What sort of question is that? I am who I am, in this time or any other time for that matter. If you must know my name is Thomas, this is my cottage, and we are all in Thorncombe Wood.'

Amelie was looking around, with a faint feeling of recognition.

'Esme, we have been here, you remember…. we came a few years ago.'

Luka was looking around too, and he nodded, almost to himself.

'You're the writer chap aren't you.'

Thomas Hardy smiled and ushered them inside.

'We have been upstairs here, but we had to get a ticket.' Their host looked confused, Luka carried on regardless 'Smelled of damp and it was gloomy. There were people and they dressed up.... Well.... Just like you really.'

Inside was a small room with a stone floor and a blazing fire. It was very cozy.

'Well to what do I owe this pleasure?' He counted. 'Four strange children at my door in the middle of the night. I assume you are lost.'

'Well yes and no, err,' Amelie stumbled and tried to find the right words to describe how they were here, but she couldn't. Would you have done any better?

Yaya chipped in. 'We are in the middle of an adventure, and it makes very little sense, but it is something to do with a quest and fairies.'

'Yes, and we keep meeting strange famous people who are all really fairies like I expect you are'. Added Esme still clutching her sword.

'Well, I am a storyteller by trade but this one is beyond my own imagination. But I do know children, so I suspect you are hungry.' He paused, 'I have just had supper with some of my favourite characters and there is enough left over to satisfy most appetites.' He called out 'Hey Jude, Tess,

Bathsheba we have guests.'

Luka suddenly began to sing, and what voice! None of them (except perhaps Yaya) had any idea he had such a talent. His voice was so crystal clear, and the audience was captured from the first note, gripped, and haunted simultaneously, the song rose as if on angel wings.

"Hey Jude, don't make it bad.

Take a sad song and make it better.

Remember to let her into your heart,

Then you can start to make it better.

Hey Jude, don't be afraid.

You were made to go out and get her.

The minute you let her under your skin,

Then you begin to make it better.

And anytime you feel the pain, hey Jude, refrain,

Don't carry the world upon your shoulders.

For well you know that it's a fool who plays it cool

By making his world a little colder.

Hey Jude, don't let me down.

You have found her, now go and get her.

Remember to let her into your heart,

Then you can start to make it better.

So let it out and let it in, hey Jude, begin,

You're waiting for someone to perform with.

And don't you know that it's just you, hey Jude, you'll do,

The movement you need is on your shoulder.

Hey Jude, don't make it bad.

Take a sad song and make it better.

Remember to let her under your skin,

Then you'll begin to make it

Better better better better better better, oh.

Na na na nananana, nannana, hey Jude..."

Luka stopped and seemed embarrassed.

'Er…. sorry, don't know what came over me.' He looked around and shuffled uncomfortably.

Mr Hardy was in tears, Amelie and Esme were staring at him open mouthed when the staggeringly beautiful Bathsheba came over, gave him a wordless hug, and a sloppy great kiss on his forehead.

After a period of utter silence, Tess D'Urberville asked in awe, 'Did you write that?'

'No' said Luka 'it was a beetle called Paul.'

Chapter 33

Magical Wanderings

Supper was rustic, simple, and quite magical. Amelie was the only one who had read any of Thomas Hardy's stories, the one about Tess. She knew that Tess had died at the end of that story but here she was eating baked potatoes and cheese with her. A loud knocking stopped her getting tangled in her thoughts.

Mr Hardy grumbled about getting no peace and the miserable looking and slightly out of focus Jude went to see who it was. He opened the door and could not initially see anyone, till he looked down, and saw a large hare staring at him.

'Ruddy heck, it's a big bunny.'

'A hare I'll have you know.'

'Get uppity with me and I'll have you jugged.'

'You will have to catch me first and some obscure little pipsqueak like you ain't fast enough.'

Jude took a kick, but the hare dodged it easily.

Yaya jumped up.

'Stop it, stop it, he's our friend, Liplop…. That is you isn't it.?'

The hare stayed outside, eying Jude warily, and addressed Yaya.

'Of course it's me, but youse all needs to get a move on, not a time for fraternisin' with imaginary folk in a queer old cottage. The fairies are gatherin' and tis best you were there. I knows not why, but tis best, you mark my words, come on …. time to go.'

'Sorry Mr Hardy and all but if Liplop says we must, then we must.' Said Yaya.

The children all got up and were soon outside with Liplop. They followed him to the bottom of the garden path and turned back to wave, but all was dark. They could only just make out the cottage but there were no lights. A large barn owl hooting nearby made them jump and swooped over them a little too low for comfort. Liplop chattered his teeth at the bird with obvious distaste and headed upwards into a very dark wood.

'Blimey, it's really dark, magically dark I expect, stay close kids, don't want anyone getting lost does we, eh?'

The trees were close around them, branches feeling for them, it did not feel friendly, there were creaks, shrieks, and horrid silences but Liplop pressed on. Even Esme's sword gave almost no light. They were still travelling uphill, the pace was fast, suddenly there was a splash and a bit of hairy cursing.

'Bother, bummer and buckytruckies....' Or something like that. 'STOP! ....'

Everyone did, suddenly the moon appeared at their feet, from behind the clouds which had suddenly departed. The wonderfully battered yellow image of Earth's first satellite was reflected in a small lake of incredible blackness.

Liplop had taken a step backwards and was shaking his big tub thumping feet to get rid of clingy wet mud, in so doing everyone around him were getting covered in the stuff. There was much shouting, waving of arms and soon general hilarity. The evil forest's spell was well and truly broken. Esme's sword had regained its gleam and she was waving it around her head in glee.

'Oooh heck, now what?' said Liplop. They all looked where he was looking. There was another gleaming sword coming up the far side of the hill, friend, or foe they wondered.

It was Amelie with her love of horses that sensed rather than saw what is was. She stared, her jaw dropped, and she gasped.

'It's not a sword it's a horn! A Unicorn....

look…look…it is! It's a Unicorn!'

They looked and it was…… even Liplop was awestruck, not able to believe his magical eyes. This wonderful mythical creature, the size of a large horse, stood across the water, whiter than any description of white, and with a single gleaming horn.

There were several large red mushrooms at his feet, covered in white dots, which the Unicorn ate quite casually while keeping his gaze on the group across the water.

'They are Fly Agaric toadstools' said Luka with his usual unwavering authority.

'He'll be flying soon if'n yer right, fairies won't like it mind you, they be fairy mushrooms if'n yer listen to the old stories'. Added Liplop.

'He is a unicorn you idiots and must know what he is doing for heaven's sake.'

Exclaimed Amelie with some irritation and headed off in the direction of this amazing creature. He watched her come and stood his ground. Amelie ruffled his long mane and was nuzzled in reward.

'Er…. Mr Unicorn…do you talk? All the animals round here seem to so …well … I just wondered if you do.'

After a long silence the unicorn spoke in a deep horsey sort of voice.

'I live in a stable, when I am able, a creature of fable but not under the table, I am a sort of horse, for better or worse, but I never liked gorse of course. I like my corn, and when I was born, I am often forlorn and torn but God gave me a horn, a unique horn, so me? I'm a unicorn. Now begone.' Finishing his curious monologue with a loud snuffly neighing.

'Blimey… those mushrooms have done 'im no good.' Said Liplop rolling his eyes.

Esme and Yaya both giggled at the obviously intellectually challenged magical creature. Amelie was crestfallen but hugged him, he might not be brainy, but he was unquestionably beautiful.

They became aware of another sound. It took a while to identify what it was, but…. yes… it was marching feet, lots of marching feet, lots and lots of marching feet.

'Romans!' yelled Luka 'Coming right for us.'

Far down the hill, on side of the Unicorn, they could see a long, long column of marching soldiers, the moonlight shining from their burnished breastplates and shining from the tips of spears. What a sight!

Liplop knew. 'Oh heck, t'is the old roman road, allus

said to be haunted but never seen it afore…. Look kids, just stand quiet and they won't do no 'arm, they are not of our time.'

Yaya wrinkled her brow wondering what was their time. They seemed to be dotting all over the place.

Soon the first romans breasted the hill, the unicorn whinnied, reared up, at which Amelie fell backwards into a bush, and galloped off. Then…. well the strangest thing…… in a very strange night. The soldiers marched through the pond…… but half of their bodies were submerged. Soon the leading column had disappeared into the earth. Luka concentrating hard was counting. The column didn't seem to be getting any shorter.

'It's a Legion, it is, I think it is the Second Augustus legion because they have goats on their shields. Must be about 90AD.'

'The lake was lower then, obviously.'

Yaya added, not to be outdone by her know it all brother.

Esme nervously edged nearer to the soldiers, and tried to tap them with her sword, but it was just empty air. The soldiers were just phantasms condemned to march the same road for all eternity. Suddenly feeling very sorry for them she hoped they did not realise their fate.

'I think the road is where we have to go.'

And the hare hopped off down the hill just to the side of the now silent marching men, all with fixed grim battle hardened faces and steely determination in their eyes.

After quite a way the last few carts and stragglers from legion disappeared up the hill and they came to a long very misty marshy lake. Esme vaguely recognised it and shook her somewhat bush scratched sister.

'Look this is that nice place with the big house. Kingston something.'

'Only there is no big house, or if there is I can't see it in this murk, and it is not nice now.'

Replied Amelie, still in a grump because of the disappearance of the unicorn.

'Don't you remember, there was statue of an arm with a sword coming out of this lake, must have been meant to be Excalibur, what a coincidence now we are having this adventure.' No reply was forthcoming.

Suddenly a strange compulsion came over Esme, and she stopped, looked into the water, and threw her magic sword in a large curving arc into the lake. Shall we let Tennyson take over.

'But ere he dipt the surface, rose an arm clothed in white samite, mystic, wonderful, and caught him by the hilt, and brandished him three times, and drew him under in the mere.'

Chapter 34

The Horrid Hillfort

Yaya was thinking about time, and her brain was hurting. Ever since they had begun this adventure time had been all over the place...... going backwards.... going forwards...... but at least so far...... not into the future. She was at the back of the little group and suddenly saw Esme, about ten metres ahead, throw her sword. Why? ......she was even more amazed at the magical arm that emerged from the foggy lake...... but still why? It was such a special possession, surely far too valuable to throw away like that.

After the arm had waved three times and slid back under the water everyone was stood still watching the ripples spread out, it was very.... very quiet....and then it wasn't.

There was a deep gurgling sound and a huge helmet with feathers like horns began to emerge from the spot where the magical arm had been. A mumbling of cross, not quite intelligible speech accompanied the huge, armoured figure who appeared from the lake waving a very small sword.

'Harrumph, wrong ruddy sword, that's not my sword, it's all flipping mixed up.' Or something like that said the obviously angry figure. The girls knew him at once.

'It is King Arthur!' they said as one.

The huge shining figure stared at them, and suddenly recognition flashed across his face.

'Yaya, is that you?'

She nodded and smiled at the not so small triumph of being remembered by such a mighty king. Arthur seemed genuinely relieved.

'Oh, thank heavens, you will be able to explain what is going on and where my duty lies.'

Panic enveloped her, as you know she hadn't a clue, but she was thinking, fast as she could. Arthur was by now stepping out of the lake and towering over her, dripping a little. Yaya stared at him wondering what she could say, then relief flooded over her. She spotted the solution.

'Sir, I think that is your sword by your side.' She pointed at the sheathed Excalibur. Arthur looked to check.

'Oh....er...yes.... you seem to be right little maid.' He said grasping the hilt to check it really was there.

'Then whose is this one?' He waved Esme's about.

'Mine...mine...' cried you know who, and he handed

it gently back to her.

'Esme, isn't it? I am confused in time and space but at least I recognise you too, and …. Amelie…. but where is Merlin?'

Everyone instinctively looked around, realised that was silly and stood nervously waiting for Arthur to do something. Luka noticed that Liplop had vanished, the mist was clearing, and the sun was about to come up. There across the lake, above a large sloping lawn, stood the huge white mansion that was Kingston Maurward House, soon illuminated by the first rays of the morning sun. Arthur's armour shone too, making him a truly awe inspiring sight.

'They should put a statue here to commemorate this.' Said Luka.

'I am sure they will.' Said a smiling Yaya.

King Arthur was very restless, pacing up and down, waiting for Merlin or Morgana to guide him. Then, apparently deciding on a course of action, he strode off without a backward glance. Very purposively in the direction they had just come from. The children watched him go, but no one fancied going backwards, so quickly he was out of sight.

Liplop seemed to appear out of thin air.

'Gone, has he? Beware of mythical kings is my motto, get you into all sorts of trouble. An' as for you Esme we would all be grateful if'n you stops throwin' your sword about. Obviously upsets the neighbours.'

He set off at a fair pace with his followers doing just that. Very soon the dramatic shape that was Maiden Castle loomed out of the landscape. They crossed the empty Weymouth road and began climbing. Liplop hesitated, twitched his whiskers, seeming uncertain.

'The magic is not right here'…. he sniffed the air…. 'perhaps tis the Pummery fort you should be goin' to?'

The children became a little nervous…… it was uncharacteristic of the hare to be uncertain. Luka had one of his 'bad feeling about this' moments.

It was still a beautiful sunny morning as they took on the slopes of the great hillfort. The size and complexity of the ditches was humbling, who had built this strange complex? A man who knew suddenly appeared in front of them. This time shimmering, not solid, but clearly Sir Mortimer Wheeler.

'Wrong time wrong place kids, make a run through the East Gate, past the temple and down the midsection. Not a good time to be here....er.... good luck.'

With that worrying warning he flickered and vanished. Liplop was wild eyed and obviously distressed. Suddenly a man wearing very primitive clothes rushed out of the ruined gate now in front of them, he didn't seem to see them. Luka, who was in front, tried to dodge him only for him to run right through him. A thin stick like object was flying in a huge arc towards the fleeing man. There was a thud and the man fell dead in front of them with a huge spear protruding from his back. The girls screamed, the man flickered, became a skeleton, and disappeared into the earth. More ghosts of the past. Luka knew that same skeleton was now in the Dorchester museum, spearpoint still there. He shivered....it is a very odd feeling when a ghost runs through you.

The weather was changing rapidly. What was at one moment a warm sunny autumn day was changed utterly by the arrival of an evil looking low, and very black cloud. Suddenly it was freezing, then a horrid, vicious, hailstorm lashed them out of nowhere. The children were stung by the blitz of sharp little ice balls but there was nowhere to shelter.

Liplop, to give him credit, did not flee but tried to

guide everyone off the hillfort. With his help they reached the remains of Danu's temple, now outlined in white. The wind rose and the hail was replaced by driving snow, it was a blizzard, a whiteout! They could not see anything.

Huddling together as best they could in the ruins of the little old temple, they were sure they were going to die here…. the wind howled…. huge snowflakes lashed their faces and if anyone spoke ….no one could hear them. Almost unconsciously they formed a circle looking inwards, arms wrapped over the one opposite, with Liplop in the middle. They were soon covered in a few inches of snow, like an instant igloo, then the noise abated. Silence took over. Except they became aware of the hare chanting,

'Nasagwagusa…... isawagusainai…...
gogonainai…... gogonanarada…...
nabwibwi……nabjibibonggong!

Bulegalegisa……bulegalegisa…...bulegalegisa…...
bulegalegisa……...'

It was Luka who first noticed it was getting warmer. Shaking his head to get rid of the snow he looked up ……they were no longer outside …. this was a familiar place…. well to him…. the temple was back.

He shouted. 'We're ok, we're ok, it's Danu's temple. It's back. Well done, Liplop, well done.'

The hare looked a bit bashful and relieved at the same time, the children pulled apart and looked round. Amelie shrieked as she saw the statue of Diana pointing her bow and arrow straight at her, but there was no Danu this time. A shimmering oval mirror hung on the back wall. Liplop pointed to it and gestured for them to go in that direction.

Esme took no persuading, and the others followed. They all stopped at the mirror and looked at their reflections, now what? It must be a magic mirror, like the one Alice went through she thought, poking her sword at it. There was a flash, she felt an electric shock shoot up her arm, and she dropped the weapon. The mirror dissolved into blackness, everyone ran through, leaving Esme now last after scrabbling to pick up her precious possession.

They found themselves in another long, dark, steeply descending, very damp smelling tunnel. After quite a while they appeared to reach the bottom and started to climb again. It seemed a long way but eventually there was an open door.... they found themselves in an almost normal room with sofas, and some sandwiches on a table. A rather smart door was at the far end. Yaya tried the handle only to find it locked. They all sat down.... ate.... and immediately fell asleep.

Time passed.... no one knew how much...... they

woke up.... one by one. Liplop had gone.

Yaya was thinking aloud.

'So, some of this is real, and we are all four together, which we were not at the start. And we are not at the Grandfolks home......I believe we are under the hill fort and that time is all mixed up....and that the fairies or whoever are hoping we can help them get it back in order......or something like that.'

Luka felt in his pocket, yes, the fairy knife was still there too. It was a little bit blue. There was magic around.

The smart door clicked open, with a sound like space airlocks in movies.... ssshhhh stccck.... another tunnel.... but this was very smart tunnel. It was more a tube really, very space age, the walls were smooth, shiny, but not metal.

Voices were in their heads. Whispering, chattering, all around them, even inside them. Looking around they saw nothing except this all-embracing soft orange light.

Instinctively everyone knew it was the fairies, this was their place, wherever and whenever that was. The tunnel slowly tipped and split.... there was a choice of direction up or down.

Luka suggested they split, two go up and two go

down, but Amelie would have none of it.

'We were told not to separate; we must stay as one.'

The others agreed.

'Ok, well I don't fancy going down. Shame Liplop has disappeared.' Grumbled Luka.

So they went up. The chattering continued; some words were almost understandable…. almost. After a while a small cat appeared walking in the same direction as them.

The cat stopped and for no very good reason they stopped too. He turned and everyone stared at him…. he was very battered…. half an ear was missing…. his fur was burned in patches…… he looked half dead really…. and about one hundred years old!

Speaking, in a very croaky, scrapy, catty, German sort of voice, he said.

'I am Schrödinger. I may be alive, I may be dead, even I don't know, so you definitely don't know, that is the only definite thing in the universe.'

'Oh heavens!' Thought Yaya 'Another impossible animal.'

'You are famous, but you aren't called Schrödinger,

you belong to him, well sort of.' Exclaimed Amelie, the oldest of course. 'You are in my physics book, something to do with quantums and probability. You don't really exist; you are an idea not a thing.'

And the cat vanished. Esme looked thoughtful.

'I think he disappeared because you didn't believe in him, like Mr Brunel. So......do we believe in Fairies? I think that is what all this might be about.'

The chattering in their heads was getting louder and more urgent.

'Well, I certainly didn't' Said Luka 'But after all we have been through it is very hard not to. So, are we all agreed that yes, we do believe in fairies?'

Everyone nodded.

The light changed instantly, and in front of them was a circular door that filled the tunnel. Purplish and very intricate. Yaya saw that it was two intertwined snakes forming shimmering and changing patterns.

 As she gazed, hypnotised by the moving patterns it was soon obvious that they weren't snakes but dragons!

A familiar male voice half whispered.

'We were the Dragon Lords of Anu, the Tuatha, last of the great fairy race and you are welcome to our meet.'

The door opened soundlessly, and there they were...... a myriad of fairy creatures...... suddenly silent ....and all staring at them.

Chapter 35

The Fairies and Arthur

The children could not take them all in. The room, if it was a room, was filled with figures.

Some like they imagined fairies to be, small delicate fine boned and beautiful. But there were others, centaurs, half men half horse, minotaurs, half bull half horse. Unicorns, goat men with horns, green men with faces of leaves, and in the far distance giants, trolls and yes...... dragons!

The trouble was that when you looked directly at anyone or anything it became blurred, slightly out of focus and indistinct. It was only at the edges, out the corner of their eyes, that these creatures were clearer. Perhaps humans are not designed to see undisguised fairies directly.

In the distance framed in an orange glow, a lady sat at table.... she stood.... and Luka knew her. Automatically, without thinking, he dropped to one knee. The others noticed and stood rooted to the spot.

Yaya wondered if she should bow or curtsey, Amelie and Esme just stared.

Luka, in a loud stage whisper,

'That is Danu, she is the goddess, she is the Queen!'

And gazed, doe eyed at this vision of loveliness.

'Only of the Tuatha.'

Said a perky little voice. Esme turned and saw a young girl with long golden hair to her feet, smiling at her. The girl laughed, a tinkling delicious happy sort of laugh. Esme knew who she was.

'You are Belli.'

'And you are no nitwit.'

'Edgar was upset you didn't come.'

'I did, he just didn't recognise my Mary Anning impression.'

That laugh again.

'Me, I am a rebel fairy. I mean we are all of the same race, what is the point of exaggerating our differences instead of stressing our similarities. Daft I say.'

There was a fanfare of trumpets. Danu stood up,

'Oh, here goes...... the Queen's Xmas message! This could go on for days.'

Giggled the irreverent Belli.

'Shhh.'

Said Luka still staring adoringly at his beloved Danu.

Yaya had spotted the fairy too, but of course had no idea who she was. Belli winked at her. She reflexly smiled and tried a not very successful wink back.

The Queen was greeting the assembled company…. her soft melodious voice was in all their heads, but after a while Esme reckoned Belli did have a point…...she was still introducing everyone present…...yet she had already been talking for several minutes.

'When is she going to say anything?'

She said aloud to no one in particular. Amelie, a stickler for being correct, glared at her sister and was annoyed that she did not even seem to notice. There was a silence…. the queen had paused.

'And now I must introduce the four human children, they have travelled long and difficult journeys to be here. Shown courage above what we have come to expect and may still help us in our hour of need.'

She pointed at them; all heads turned to look…... some of them very strange heads indeed. Luka, pleased to be recognised, sort of waved as if to loyal subjects. Yaya tried to be invisible, and the sisters just stood looking a bit awkward. Yaya tried looking around a bit to take her mind off all the unwanted attention.

It was clearer now; it was a round room they were in, but an odd one. The walls were almost transparent and if she tried, she could see outside in a dim sort of way, after moments of straining and staring hard...... she knew where they were!

This was the round barrow in the Poundbury hill fort. Which either meant they were all very small or this was another extra dimensional Tardis like space.

Suddenly, just as the queen was talking about love, kindness, and harmony it went quite dark. A shimmering blue sort of dark. Luka felt stung, this was the same feeling he had in the temple on Maiden Castle, perhaps it was the same time?

Someone brushed past them, almost knocking Amelie over.

'Oooh heck...now the fat is in the fire.' Squeaked Belli.

As a large, tall, greenish glowing lady strode towards Danu.

There was a lot of fairy screaming. It was much lighter now but still bluish green. Another lady wearing tweeds and with a gladstone bag nearly took Luka's head off.

He of course recognised both. The others just knew that this was the other queen and her henchwoman. This was a fairy war...... and they were in the middle of it!

'Catherine, Queen of the Formorians, you are not invited or welcome here.'

Said Danu, her voice much less soft, almost harsh.

'Well, here I am anyway.'

She sounded self-confident and very superior. There was a sound of weapons being drawn and taking up military drill positions. The children looked back to see rank upon rank of armoured elf soldiers, spears gleaming a flickering green, and archers with full quivers and bows at the ready.

'Draw.'

She commanded and her archers took their arrows and drew their bows. There was a little more screaming, but it soon died away, and then there was silence.

'In case you are interested Danu they are all aiming at you. They are special arrows and besides making you look like a demented hedgehog will keep you trapped for a thousand fairy years.'

'Gosh, that's a long time' whispered Belli.

'A fairy year is a hundred of yours.'

Luka was suddenly indignant; he was a little bit in love with Danu, so this was a crime!

He began running towards her, knocking the gladstone bag out of the doctor's hand, and bumping hard into the green queen. She was not expecting such an event and, unprepared, fell over in an undignified manner. Wriggling on the ground in a swirl of bottoms, arms, and very long legs.

There was a smattering of laughter. He reached Danu and stood as if her bodyguard. Jaw jutting and defiant. The other three, seeing Luka in the line of fire, ran to him and stood looking back at the archers.

The green queen was back on her feet, her pride severely dented. The children held their breath. Luka gulped, the thought of a thousand arrows being loosed in their direction was not the best feeling they had ever had. Behind them Danu was unbowed. Suddenly growing in size and speaking out loud, not in their heads, real speech.

'Arthur, King of Kings, I call on you to fulfil your oath. England is in peril, you are needed…...now!'

As is fitting in all such stories there was sudden

thunder and lightning then darkness fell.

There was a clanking of armour, a shuffling, and a squeaking, as those in the way tried to avoid getting trodden on.

It was obvious to the children immediately that something was wrong with the scale. This huge silver figure was just too big. Compared to them he was 30 perhaps 40 metres tall.

As you know magic is just science we don't understand. That something was wrong was obvious…. but what? ….. was much less clear.

Arthur looked around. As a magical mythical figure of legend, he was confused. He had been summoned by an unbreakable oath and knew he would have to do his duty. The trouble was he did not know what that entailed.

He was a noble king of ancient lineage and had fought many battles to make the world a better place. In his own mind he had always tried to do the right thing, even if that involved chopping off the heads of wrong (missing) headed others who wanted the opposite.

'Be sure you are right then go ahead.'

Was his motto.

Knowing what was right had not always been that easy but wise council from Merlin and Morgana Le Fey put him straight. They didn't seem to be here at this moment, and here he was with his head poking out of a large mound in a muddy field.

He looked around, fields and a river valley in front. He looked behind. Lots of new strange looking towers and palaces, but slowly he recognised where he was. There was the old Maidun fort and here was his old Camelot. Much changed but clearly recognisable.

What was he supposed to do?

Whoever had summoned him didn't seem to be here. There were no obvious heads to remove. In his experience a spectacular show often got things going, so he unsheathed Excalibur and waved it around his head, roaring in an appropriately warrior king manner.

'For England, my England.'

This deafened the unnoticed company below him, who all held their hands over their ears.

A strange magical cart appeared in front of him, covered in writhing mystic runic writing. There was a man peering out of the side of it. Arthur felt he knew him but couldn't quite place him, then he remembered.

'Mundi, it's you! I thought I had done for you.'

'Want an ice cream? The 99's are especially good.'

Chapter 36

Peace at last.

Catherine, the Formorian Queen, was pushing through towards Danu. The archers were wavering, unsure now that their own queen was coming into the firing line. As she got close, they put their bows down. The children were very relieved.

'Ooh I thought I was going to be a pincushion.'

Yaya said to Esme.

Amelie, getting braver by the minute turned to Danu.

'I think your trick has backfired. If that giant is Arthur, he is just too big to be any use.'

Danu, Queen of half the Fairies, most beautiful woman in the world was not used to being questioned by anyone, especially a stroppy Australian teenager. Her mask slipped a little.

'Who are you to question me! I was just doing what was best.'

'She's right you idiot.'

It was an angry Catherine, Queen of the other half, still several yards distant.

'This huge clodhopper you have conjured up will be

the death of all of us, and he won't even notice!'

There was more than a grain of truth in this statement and Danu knew it. Arthur shifted his feet and 100 fairy creatures fled in panic, a few didn't make it, squished like ants on a path.

There was a booming sound above, too deep, and loud to make sense of but they realized that Arthur was talking, presumably to someone. Then a loud jingly tune belted out.

'That's an ice cream van.'

Luka yelled and was suddenly chilled when he realised it was playing The Teddy Bears Picnic. The words ran through his head.

'If you go down in the woods today, you'd better not go alone

It's lovely down in the woods today, but safer to stay at home

For every bear that ever there was

Will gather there for certain because

Today's the day the teddy bears have their picnic'

'Rex Mundi! He's here, he is going to hypnotise Arthur and ....'

He wasn't sure what would happen but was pretty

certain whatever it was would not be good.

The two queens met and stared each other in the eye. A hush fell over all the fairies. Catherine spoke first.

'This is your mess Danu; I should leave you to sort out your own muddle, but you never were good at clearing up after you. You need my help, my sister, as you have so often before.'

'That's wrong! You were always a goody two shoes and mum always took your side.'

'They are sisters!'

Emily shouted to no one in particular. Luka was disappointed that his secret love was proving not quite so perfect. Yaya was just hoping they could sort out their quarrel and then they could all get on with their holiday. Amelie was wondering what was coming next and was there any way she could speed it all up a bit?

'Look you two queens, can't you just make up your differences, call off your army and work out the magic between yourselves. It shouldn't be that hard.'

There was a little clap next to her ear.

'Well said' whispered the little golden-haired fairy.

The two fabulous fairy sisters hesitated, moved awkwardly about each other, and suddenly threw themselves into an intense embrace with both in tears.

That this was a very significant moment everyone in that room knew...... well except King Arthur of course. His day was not going well.

He had tried to hit Rex Mundi's van with his sword but there was some sort of force field and Excalibur, magical though it was, had just bounced off. Rex had put his tongue out, put his fingers in his ears and done a ya boo sucks gesture before turning on his teddy bear chime and driving off.

Arthur realised he was effectively trapped, the top half of him poking out of the round barrow while his feet were in the fairy chamber. He began to struggle to free himself causing mayhem down below.

A couple of chaps in high vis jackets approached. Arthur did not know what to make of them. They obviously weren't noble knights, but if they were peasants, and he suspected they were, they were out of his usual experience. They began speaking in an unfamiliar tongue, being a creature of myth and legend, he sort of understood, but not very well.

'Oi Guv, we saw you trying to hit that ice cream bloke with that sword thing of yours. That is unfriendly and downright dangerous. My mate has called the rozzers.'

'Ere Bert, 'e seems stuck and is wearing all that tin stuff.'

'That's armour that is, must be in the pantomime, but how 'as he got half buried? Have you called 999 Geoff?'

'Well, we might need the ambulance not just the police. He looks stuck good an' proper.'

Arthur, not famous for his patience, began bellowing.

'Get me out of this ditch. You there, as your king I order you to help.'

'Oooh, order, eh? Hark at him Geoff. Delusions of grandeur too. Thinks he's king, wonder what Charles feels about that?'

Arthur was by this time getting really mad, and of course with all the magic that surrounded him that was liable to produce unexpected and catastrophic results.

Well, it did.

Bert and Geoff's white van disappeared in a lightning thunderbolt, reappeared seconds later as a charred burned-out wreck.

The police car, travelling up the road, siren blaring, took off Harry Potter like, flew gracefully over Arthur, and descended gently into the river Frome below. Fortunately, the occupants were fine if a little damp.

The two workmen were a little dispirited at seeing the smoking ruins of their van and very discombobulated by seeing a flying squad car. This mad tin man was obviously worthy of a bit more respect than they had assumed.

'Er look Guv, that's our livelihood you just blew up. We'll be expecting some compensation you know.'

But the fight had gone out of them really. Arthur stared at them, about as confused as they were.

'Help me....'

He muttered in a deeper but more conciliatory tone.

'Put that sword thing down and we'll try and get you out.'

And he did and they did.

With one on each side and a couple of good pulls he was soon on the side of the barrow. He lay briefly in an undignified heap but quickly pulled himself together. He picked up Excalibur and adopted a more kingly posture. His armour was mud streaked but still undeniably impressive, finding he was a good two foot taller than his reluctant helpers cheered him up no end.

'Cor, maybe he is some sort of king, certainly looks the part.'

'He looks a bit how you would imagine King Arthur to look I reckon, if he was real, I mean.'

Bert tailed off and kept staring.

'King Arthur!! That is who I am!!'

'Mad as a hatter.' Said Geoff but Bert was not so sure.

Arthur was looking round, getting his bearings from the old landscape that hadn't changed much. Suddenly he marched off purposively, as was his wont, in the direction of the new Poundbury on the hill.

Bert and Geoff had learned enough by now to not interfere, but they seemed driven to follow him. He strode past the great field, past a strange wooden construction covered in screaming children, and up Peverell Avenue till he was standing staring at a statue of a Queen. She had a distinctive hat and stood on a plinth in the middle of a road. He failed to notice the collection of curious children following him like the Pied Piper.

Poking at the base with his sword for no obvious reason he then slumped down on the step with head in hand. This was the right place, he was certain of that, but it was so changed. Getting up and walking slowly round the statue he gazed at her, wondering who she was.

She was certainly not his faithless Guinevere, but she did look a great queen. The magnificent buildings around him did have an echo of his fabled Camelot too. The two men in their strange orange glowing jackets were watching him, and he was suddenly aware of this cavalcade of chattering children gawping at him.

'It was here.'

He cried in a kingly theatrical voice. This stopped several pedestrians who too began gathering to stare at this strange knight in armour.

'It was here!' he repeated for emphasis.

At last Bert summoned up the necessary courage.

'What was?'

'Why my round table you fool. My round table!'

The crowd tittered. This was fun, an unexpected performance by some Amateur Dramatic society was what most of them thought.

As a King he was used to awe and deference, not being giggled at by mere subjects. Waving his sword, in a 'listen to me you fools' gesture and in his anger raising the magic.

Excalibur hit the plinth, there was a tremendous crash, a flash, and the Queen on the plinth teetered, tilted tantalisingly close to falling while Arthur desperately tried to save her. He failed, there was a gasp of shock from the assembled watchers, while Elizabeth Bowes Lyon, Queen Mother of the great Elizabeth the second.... fell off!

'Oooh heck. He's done it now. There's going to be trouble about this.'

Said Bert.

Chapter 37

A Toppled Queen

The children were of course entirely unaware of these dramatic events.

The botched conjuring up of the great king and his subsequent scrabbling around had done a great deal of damage. But something good...... even great...... had come out it.... the Fairie Queens were reconciled!

There was no longer a fairy war, hopefully this meant that these strange disturbances in time and space would come to an end.

Esme was pleased that everything had calmed down but noticed her sword had had lost its lustre. She was suddenly worried.

'Everyone listen, I think we need to get out of here as quick as we can. We were needed in some sort of way, but I think it is over now yet here we are in some place where the powers are fading, if my sword is anything to go by.'

Luka scrabbled for his Fairy knife, it was dull and blunt.

'Is it just me or is everything just getting a bit blurred and fuzzy.'

Amelie wondered aloud.

It was true, Yaya had to wrinkle her nose and squint just to see around her, and it was also getting cold.

'Hurry everyone, I think we must join hands so that whatever happens involves us all.'

So, they did and not a moment too soon. There was a buzzing as of bees, a noise they had heard before, then everything became blurred. They knew they were travelling but where? Four pairs of hands gripped each other very tightly.

'Look out, look out!'

They heard a voice (Bert's actually) and Esme saw a large statue about to roll over on them. She pulled Luka and Amelie's hand and they in turn rapidly pulled Yaya out of the way of the rolling statue.

The Queen Mother, for it was she, finally came to rest against the wall of Bowes Lyon house. Which was very appropriate as the building was named after her.

A large out of place hare scuttled away from danger and looked back to see everyone was alright. Yaya saw him and waved.

Esme's jaw dropped as she saw King Arthur. He looked a bit lost, sad, and on his own, so without thinking she rushed up to him.

He looked at this child … it was the sword that he recognised. He was pleased to see someone that he had seen before, it restored some fortitude to his veins. Her name came to him.

'Esme is that you?'

She nodded and took his hand. He was touched. He spotted the other two girls.

'You freed me from the spell.'

Looking at Yaya and Amelie. They approached him, a little nervously. They were aware how great he really was.

Luka had no idea. Nobody had talked about Arthur at his school in Croatia, so he was only very dimly aware that he was a famous old king of England. But he felt sorry for him, the king certainly seemed a bit lost and forlorn.

He gathered with the girls.

'My brother.' Said Yaya by way of introduction.

There were tears in the old king's eyes. In this incarnation he was not in the first flush of youth. The crowd began to disperse, the fun seemed to be over, just a few remained to see if anything else interesting might happen.

'This was my Camelot…'

He said almost in a whisper. Well, that is what they heard, he actually said Cavalon, but their brains translated it into what they knew. So Poundbury was definitely built on the site of Arthur's fabled City. Well, well, well.

'My Round Table, twas here, here where we sit. Equal! All my knights were equal. Clever idea was it not? I of course did have a throne and placed the knights I did not especially like away from me. Particularly that treacherous preening mountebank Lancelot'

He was getting louder, and then his mood seemed to lighten, and he chuckled,

'So, you could say all the knights were equal, but some were more equal than others.'

Amelie thought that she had heard that same idea somewhere before. But couldn't quite remember where. Arthur raised himself, sheathed his sword and spread his arms for emphasis.

'The table was here.'

And some magic happened because the table suddenly was there.

The Queen Mother statue had, until the recent

disaster, stood on a grand plinth but was in the middle of a main road and had become a somewhat confusing roundabout. This roundabout had just instantly transformed into a shiny, smooth, and huge marble topped table of precisely the same dimensions.

Arthur was now standing in the centre, the children smoothly glided to the edge and dropped onto the road. They retreated a little distance, being unsure of what was going to happen next. That was the right thing to do.

Solid unadorned oak chairs materialised; Luka counted twenty five of them. One of them was indeed bigger than the others and carved. The three large gold shields matched those on the king's breastplate.

The crowd was assembling again, most assumed this was some clever laser show, magic is not the first thing that comes to mind to a generation about to learn to live with artificial reality.

Figures were appearing on the chairs; the king jumped from the table and took sat in his throne. Men in light gleaming armour shimmered as if they were a projection. The small crowd hushed and gawped.

Esme for no good reason except that it seemed

right, waved her sword, it was shining again, the magic was back.

But not for long. A familiar van came into view, the Teddy Bear's Picnic tune echoed all around. Old Ebenezer bear waved at Luka from the window, his big pipe was making an awful lot of smoke. Soon everything was extremely hazy, as if a fog had descended.

The round table image flickered as if a fault in the streaming and faded into the haze. Another Rex, Mundi this time, pushed the old bear away and leaned out of the window, waving a magnum in Luka's direction.

'Go away. Go away.' He shouted back.

This and Mundi's presence interfered with the magic. Arthur and his knights were gone, disappeared into the murk. A silence fell, the mist evapourated and the plinth reappeared. Some of the crowd applauded at the cleverness of the light show.

There was a loud engine noise with a lot of clanking.

A huge bulldozer appeared round the corner of Bowes Lyon house and headed for the ice cream man. Mundi took the hint and shot off happily singing about picnics and teddy bears. Ebenezer waved his pipe as a final goodbye.

Sir Mortimer climbed out of the cab winked at the children and went to inspect the fallen queen. Grandad appeared out of the passenger side, struggled to climb down till Amelie helped him.

'Oh, it is you Amelie, how wonderful!'

Then he spotted the others.

'All of you, oh thank god, Judy has been so worried'.

'So, you haven't been?'

Said Esme still holding her sword.

'Oh, you know, don't be silly'.

The old man's eyes had filled up, and he couldn't manage to get anymore words out. Yaya took his hand and he burst into tears. This was of course embarrassing, but this is just what adventurous children must put up with.

Out of view, Sir Mortimer climbed back in the cab, reversed, and then scooped up the statue into the large bucket like thing at the front. Turning very professionally and pulling a large yellow lever which instantly lifted the Queen Mother to the height of the top of the plinth.

The crowd was watching intently.

'He'll never get that upright without help.' Said Bert

'Ruddy impossible. The old fool doesn't know what he is doing I reckons.' agreed Geoff.

But the children knew that this was Sir Mortimer and that he was not exactly who he appeared to be. They suspected he might have an ace up his sleeve. He did not disappoint.

There was a buzzing as of a swarm of bees or wasps.

Bert and Geoff panicked, started waving their arms about to fend off unseen stinging insects. Other than the children the rest of the crowd did the same.

The buzzing faded away as quickly as it had come. Bert looked up.

'Here, would you look at that, e's just gone and done it hasn't he!'

And there she was, no dints, cleaned up as good as new standing where she was supposed to be and none the worse for her 'accident'.

It was over, they all knew. There was no one in the cab but there was a little tinkling voice in Esme's ear.

'Goodbye Essers, I hope you still believe in fairies when you get to your Grandad's age.'

ABOUT THE AUTHOR

Peter is a grandad. He lives in and loves Poundbury.
He has written books for doctors, three novels, and two books for his grandchildren.
This is the second.
He has an Amazon author page.
He still believes in Fairies.

Printed in Great Britain
by Amazon

18333902R00203